I0640975

Nettie Sanford

History of Marshall County, Iowa

Nettie Sanford

History of Marshall County, Iowa

ISBN/EAN: 9783337381462

Printed in Europe, USA, Canada, Australia, Japan

Cover: Foto ©Andreas Hilbeck / pixelio.de

More available books at **www.hansebooks.com**

MARSHALL COUNTY,

IOWA.

By MRS. N. SANFORD.

———◆———

CLINTON, IOWA:
LESLIE, McALLASTER & CO., PRINTERS AND BINDERS.

1867.

INTRODUCTION.

In giving this little book to the citizens of Marshall County, it may be well to say it was written under many embarrassing circumstances, and not with the intention of making any elaborate literary effort. We have only tried to show the great advance made in the wealth and prosperity of this section of Iowa — the rightful heritage of the toilers amid the rocks and sterile soil of the East; therefore, we ask the kindly consideration of the critic.

We commenced it as a pamphlet work, but many wishing it in a more permanent form, we have finally issued it to our readers in a manner better suited to their tastes.

We are much indebted to many of our prominent citizens for pecuniary help, and shall ever remember them gratefully for their kindness. Also, to the Hon. H. C. Henderson, for some of the legal points in the narration of the Marietta war; to A. J. Smith, Esq., of Timber Creek, for items connected with its history; and to K. F. Cleaver, of Vienna, for the list of her soldier dead.

NETTIE SANFORD.

CONTENTS.

—•—

CONTENTS.

HON H. C. HENDERSON.   JAMES P. SANFORD.

COL. BANBURY
IOWA 5TH

HON. G. W. RICH   M. GERHART, ESQ.

IOWA.

MUCH has been said and very much written upon the inducements that Iowa holds out to settlers, yet like the glory of the East to the Queen of sacred story, the half has not been told. The word "Iowa" in one Indian dialect means the "drowsy," and the beautiful stream bearing this name sleeps along the prairie's edge through Marshall county as if loth to leave its pleasant borders. There are wild apples and wild roses on its banks — you hear the drowsy tapping of the partridge in the cottonwoods — the drone of beetles; a little further on in a quiet bayou, there are white lilies bearing a resemblance to the ancient lotus, where wild bees are slumbering within their pearly folds; these sights and sounds to a child of nature, be he poet or Pottawatomie, have a drowsy, sweet significance in the word *Iowa*. We write the history of

MARSHALL COUNTY,

With a few statistics, to show what a wonderful progress has been made in little less than twenty years, in developing the resources and wealth of the country. We give a very short geographical delineation of Marshall. It is situated near the forty-first

2

parallel of latitude, is almost exactly in the center of
the State, twenty-four miles square, and contains
368,640 acres of magnificent land — an almost un-
broken garden through its limits. This county is
divided into sixteen civil townships, Vienna, Bangor,
Iowa, Liberty, Minerva, Marion, Le Grand, Greencastle,
Marshall, Timber Creek, Jefferson, Washington, Marietta, Eden, State Center, and one township not named.

The products are wheat, corn, rye, oats, barley,
broom-corn, sorghum, garden vegetables and wild fruit
in great profusion. Vegetables grow to an enormous
size; they would scarcely be recognized if thrown
among their poor relations of the Atlantic shore.
There are good orchards in every township, and we
will be able soon to depend upon home culture for
fruit. There are nurseries scattered all through the
county to supply farmers with young trees and cuttings,
which ought to be patronized instead of getting dry
and worthless sticks from the East. One farmer in this
section paid twenty-five dollars for Eastern fruit trees,
and received a single apple tree in the collection
that wore a leaf. All the fruits that can be grown in
this latitude, can be successfully cultivated in Iowa,
except peaches, and even these can be grown by careful culture.

There is a prejudice against our climate which is
wholly unfounded, that it is too severe for fruit—often
an excuse for idleness in the care of trees, etc. We
have cold winters but plenty of snow, and the autumns
are the very perfection of climate. The springs are
a degree warmer than New York, Northern Pennsylvania and Ohio. Flowers are peerless, both on
the prairie and in the door-yards. Hon. D. L.
Arnold received the diploma for the most tastefully
arranged garden, by the Fair committee last season.
There was a magnificent gladiolus that bloomed in
Mrs. C. B. Straight's yard in Marshalltown, the past
summer; pansies of the largest size and velvety

richness, at Mrs. H. Wiley's; and in every day beauty, glowed crimson grass pinks and larkspurs, in Mrs. Peet's yard. Nothing could surpass the beautiful collection of green-house plants at Mr. C. C. Smith's; and for evergreens, magnificent in proportion, we point to Mr. Woodbury's and Mr. Willigrod's grounds on Station street. Mrs. Bunce has a beautifully arranged flower plat also, and is very successful in the culture of strawberries. A piece of ground five feet by ten, grew the enormous quantity of twenty-four quarts of this delicious fruit at different pickings. Mr. Barnhart has been equally fortunate in strawberry raising; so that we can safely say that Iowa cannot be surpassed in this fruit, with proper culture, for in other parts of the town and county, nearly like results have been obtained. The forest is full of wild apples and plums, and honey is plentiful and cheap.

RAILROADS.

The Cedar Rapids and Missouri, sometimes called the Iowa Northwestern, is now finished to Omaha, connecting with the Union Pacific, giving railroad connection westward with the North Platte and Denver, and eastward, by car, to Chicago, and onward to the sea-girt shore. We supply many of the little towns and stations along the line with provisions, especially butter, eggs, etc. There is another road projected from Marshalltown to Eldora, which will be finished before many years.

The Pacific Telegraph, whose lines glisten west to the Sierra Nevada, and north to the new land of Sitka, passes through Marshalltown from Chicago, thus giving us lightning prescience with the world.

STONE AND TIMBER.

Freestone for building purposes is found in Le Grand, Marion; and at the corner of Timber Creek township,

is found a dark red conglomerate, which is easily
wrought, admirably adapted for foundations to buildings, wells, etc. Brick is manufactured of an excellent character here, while dressed lumber can be
obtained at our yards in unlimited amount and of
the best quality, beside that from the native forests,
making building a light matter to the settler. We
have large groves of cottonwood, oak, lime, hack-
berry, walnut, hickory, etc., which are ready for the
ax, growing like Jack's bean-stalk, in the rich soil, if
the prairie fires are kept at a respectful distance.
Coal is brought from Boone and Eldora by car and
wagons, although there is plenty of coal in the county
as will be seen under the head of the different townships, but it is not so easily worked as at the above-
mentioned places.

PASTURAGE.

The immense range of our plains is rapidly lessen-
ing, but still there is enough for stock — great plenty.
With the present efficient machinery, hay can be had
for the cutting, in the lowlands, abundantly able to
furnish feed for any amount of animals. The Marshall
County Agricultural Society has given some very
choice premiums for farm stock, so that in this
section we have some fine horses. The fastest time
made by a native, Blackhawk Tom, given by his
owner, H. Nash, was 2.49. And mules, too — fine
specimens. Swine are raised by the thousands, mostly
of an improved breed.

President Chapin of the Agricultural Society has
been very energetic in making the organization a
power for good among the farmers, and there have been
some creditable exhibitions at the Fair grounds east
of Marshalltown. But the crowning profit of agricultural investment is in sheep. Our high and dry
prairies, if the animals are protected from the cold
winds, are extremely favorable to a healthy growth.

MARSHALL WOOLEN MILLS.

The wool commands a high price at the factory of Woodbury & Son, and Eastern buyers are ready here to keep this staple at a high figure.

MANUFACTURES.

There are thirteen grist and saw mills in different parts of the county, and others in process of erection. Some of these have powerful engines, doing an immense business in flour, and building-lumber.

We have two carding machines, an iron foundry by Lockwood & Frederick, of Marshalltown, also a sash, blind and glove factory, and three broom factories, which have made in a year about twenty-two hundred dozen brooms, supplying other towns with these useful articles to a great extent. We will enumerate four carriage shops, a large plow manufactory, a chandler shop, four butcher establishments, a fanning mill factory; and Messrs. Shaw & Andrews are making a splendid article of window shades.

We have not space to particularize, but in the notice of the different townships, and city directory, the stranger may read of our unwonted prosperity in this direction. But in the factory of Mr. G. M. Woodbury & Son, is the *chef d'œuvre* of Marshalltown enterprise. It is situated near the depot, built of Le Grand free-stone, four stories, the main building eighty by fifty feet, and, with the machinery, cost about fifty thousand dollars. It runs ten looms, four hundred and fifty spindles, manufactures, daily, three hundred and fifty yards of cloth, and daily employs twenty-five persons. The building is heated throughout by the escape steam passing through pipes, and is lighted by gas generated in the building. It is a very extensive affair for the Iowa valley, and reflects great credit upon Mr. Woodbury and Son for their public spirit and energy.

In the Iowa river north of Marshalltown, there is a

water power of ten feet, already turning a grist mill, a large carding machine, saw mill, etc., and yet it is not half improved. We invite capitalists from the East to this point, and can safely insure a paying investment upon stock. An oil mill would do well here if farmers should interest themselves in flaxseed.

COMMON SCHOOLS, ETC.

No county in the State is better supplied with good schools and buildings than Marshall. There are eighty subdistricts and seventy school houses, and well furnished with the modern improvements for the benefit of the students.

School buildings are under contract in different parts of the county this coming season, which will increase our educational advantages sufficiently to meet every want of the community. Our proximity to the Agricultural College of Story county will soon be of great benefit to our people, as well as to the State at large. Teachers are well paid from the magnificent school fund, and a healthy public sentiment sustains them in all efforts to maintain discipline, and inculcate lessons of morality and religion.

MILITARY RECORD.

Marshall County has a proud record in putting down the slaveholders' rebellion, having sent over eight hundred to the grand army of the Union. This, according to her population, was a good showing of her patriotic spirit. Gloriously, the brave boys from our midst carried the old flag on the bloody fields of Pittsburg Landing, Donelson, Inka, Milliken's Bend, Champion Hills, and many, many other places, where they won a renown equal to the heroes of Marathon and Thermopylæ. But it is idle for an insignificant pen like ours to attempt to write an eulogy on Iowa soldiers. We might as well attempt to describe the Alps, or do any other impossible thing. The brave deeds of Marshall soldiers are written in blood by the Fifth, Eighth, Eleventh, Thirteenth, and Twenty-third Regiments of Iowa Volunteers. Also, in the Second Iowa Cavalry, Fourth Battery, and too, in the Eighth Cavalry, and there were a few in the Fourth Cavalry.

The prison life of some of these would fill a volume, that attests their heroic fortitude. And, first on the shining record, is Simon Woolston, of Edenville, who died in the filthy stockade of Andersonville, after eight weeks of horrible suffering from wounds, disease and starvation. He is wearing the martyr's crown with others from our regiment rolls, and may their memory be ever fragrant to a patriotic people. We must honor our returned soldiers more, cherish the memory of the lost in our heart of hearts, and build, just as soon as possible, some grand testimonial within our limits, in memory of those who gave their lives for the preservation of the Republic.

Among our citizens whom we should honor, is Colonel Banbury, Colonel Shurtz, Captain Haskins, Captains Cleavers and Page, Lieutenants Hoffman, Beeson, and the glorious rank and file, who won the battles without straps or chevrons. If there are any we have omitted here, it is for want of space; they are all good and brave; rather than detract from the fame of an Iowa soldier, let our right arm be paralyzed, and " the shoulder be broken from the bone."

In this connection, we will speak of the escape of Captain Page and Lieut. M. Hoffman from prison after thirteen months' captivity, nearly. They were taken with Sergeant Oviatt and eight men at Mission Ridge, November 25, 1863, and sent to Libby prison by way of the Southern railroads. When within a few miles of Augusta, Ga., Captain Page having made a saw from a table knife, managed to cut a hole through the bottom of the car, and drop out on the track. He eluded their pursuit five days, when he was recaptured by the bloodhounds, and was sent on with the rest to Libby prison, where he and Hoffman spent five months among the chivalry that dispensed mouldy corn-cob bread and mule meat, instead of their boasted hospitality. In the meantime Edward Bissell, one of the nine, died at Belle Island.

The fate of another of the party, Alonzo Rogers, never was known; very likely he was killed by the dogs in trying to make his escape. Three of the number were sent to Andersonville, where they died in the filthy stockade. As I look upward among the stars, I read the names of these soldier martyrs, John Miller, Charles Smith, and Andrew Heller.

On the 7th of May following, the party from Libby prison were transferred to Macon, Ga.; after spending a part of the summer in that Southern resort, they were sent to Charleston, S. C., for the humane purpose of being placed under fire for the protection of the city. But Union bullets and shells had another mission, and fortunately they escaped unhurt as the shells still screamed on over the dismantled churches, etc. Many of the prisoners dying of the yellow fever, the Marshall boys, with others, were ordered on board a train bound for Columbia, S. C. Captains Page and Hoffman again attempted an escape, but were retaken on the fourth day and placed in durance vile. While the train was moving quite slow in passing a crossing, they slipped slyly down from the open cars and crawled under the bridge till the train was out of sight, when they made for a cornfield, on the double quick. But in spite of all their precaution and ingenuity, they were brought back again under the rebel flag.

At last, in being paroled to get wood and pine brush for bedding, they made their final escape, and after thirty-five days of patient, weary travel, they reached our lines at Sweet Water, forty miles from Knoxville, Tenn. They were ragged, and their feet were sore and blistered; hungry and emaciated, they were glad to see their comrades, and the old starry banner float ing over the little station. They had no guide but the North Star and the faithful blacks, who divided food with them. Page used to sing the battle hymns of the Republic to these lowly men and women of the South, then partake of their humble food with merry laughter, having Hoffman and a certain Major for *vis a vis* companions.

Riley Westcott, now living in Wisconsin, and Charles Eagen, were left at Belle Island, but were regularly exchanged afterward.

While Captain Page was at Charleston, he sent a letter to his wife enclosed in a button of a surgeon's coat sewed on in the proper place. It gave great comfort to his anxious family although it was only four by five inches square.

Colonel Shurtz, once a private in the Mexican war, was taken prisoner at Nooney, Ga., and making his escape twice, was finally taken to Columbia, S. C. He was severely wounded in the hands, crippling him for life, yet managed to subsist on the miserable fare, when he was exchanged after five months' captivity.

Let us not forget the sufferings of these men, and when we can show our gratitude in society, in conventions, on all public occasions, let such as these take the "upper seats in the synagogue."

There was another noble, patriotic, young man who went from our midst, Martin V. B. Drum, who died after twelve months' service, at Camp Big Springs, Miss. He was buried on a bright Fourth of July morning, the thunders of the garrison pealing out that there were still brawny arms to defend the nation he had given his young life to save. He was the soul of the camp and sadly missed by his companions as they laid him down to rest under the sods of the Southern vale. *In cœlo quies.*

Perhaps there was no soldier from this county who gained promotion under prouder circumstances than Clarington Poynes. He entered Captain Page's company, a very unprepossessing private, but rose to the position of Captain after three years' service and re-enlistment in the Iowa Third Cavalry. He received his commission on the day of his death, being shot in leading his company at the taking of Nashville bridge. He had already struck down two rebels with his trusty sword.

HISTORY.

Prior to the settlement of this county by the whites, it was inhabited by the Sac and Fox tribes of Indians, remnants of the once powerful nation presided over by the far-famed Black Hawk. A portion of these Indians roving westward have returned, and now live in this and Tama county by permission of the legislature, but are nearly all incapable of civilization. They call themselves Musquaquas. In the winter of 1847, a body of Mormons in their flight from Nauvoo to Salt Lake, camped and stayed through the winter in the forest north of where Marshalltown now stands. Famine and disease attacked them and many perished, although they peeled the red elm bark for bread. In the spring following, they folded their tents and planted their church standards beyond the Big Muddy. A few stragglers remained and built cabins at Council Bluffs.

The first permanent white settler in the county was Joseph Davison, who came to Le Grand township in 1847, and very soon after, his brother, William Davison, came and built a cabin in that vicinity. But the first settlement of any size was made in Timber Creek on the south side of the grove, in 1848. The pioneers of the movement were Joseph Ferguson and Josiah Cooper. After this, a few settlers came into Iowa townships, Bangor, Marietta, and Marshall. The county was organized in 1849, J. M. Ferguson acting as sheriff, and J. Hobbs was appointed judge.

In July of 1851, the first court was held in a little log building in the edge of the forest near where Colonel Shurtz lives, the grand jury meeting in the bushes just across the slough. No bill of indictment was found, and these representatives of justice were in session only about ten minutes. How the merry squirrels and gophers must have laughed in their sleeves at the solemn faces of the jurors with nothing to do.

The First District Court was held, with Judge McKay from Des Moines, on the bench. Several lawyers of great renown, afterwards, were there. Lieutenant-Governor Eastman, in those days called "Uncle Enoch," was quite prominent in cutting hay for the horses owned by this august body, as well as expounding law and equity. Seevers, of Oskaloosa, laughed at him somewhat, telling him, with a curious leer in his eye, that he made better winrows than speeches. Cassidy, of Polk, who now ranks high in the profession, was also in attendance, and a young lawyer who never gained much distinction, by the name of Young.

As the family of Mr. William Ralls lived in the cabin there was not much room for forensic display. Mrs. Ralls cooked their meals out of doors by a chunk fire, and when night came Attorneys Eastman and Seevers were obliged to sleep in the loft, climbing up a pole ladder. Their dignity was somewhat taken down as they slowly swung themselves over the heads of the family. As Eastman went up, looking down at the cradle (rather a primitive one, made of oak shakes), " Well," said the witty lawyer, " that looks like the running gear of a whippoorwill's nest."

Zeno Freeman was treasurer. John Amos, Greenbury Ralls, and William Ballard, were county commissioners, which answered to the wants of the county in the same manner that our board of supervisors do to-day. A Mr. Walker was school fund commissioner sometime after; and Jacob Hauser was county clerk.

At this term of the court there were two cases on the docket, Higgins *v.* Smith, of Hardin county, and the divorce suit of William Davison and his wife, who were made twain, instead of *one* flesh. Mrs. Davison remarked, as her husband rode up on horseback, "La!" said she, "Old Billy thinks he's goin' to git a divorce, anyhow. See how straight he sets up."

Sometime during the summer of this year, the commissioners appointed by the legislature to locate the county seat for Marshall, passed over some very eligible locations so it was said, but finally settled on Marietta, a good deal influenced by the judgment of William Dishon, a settler in that region.

In the history of the county, we must not omit that this was the year for the highest water known since its settlement. The Iowa river was three miles wide, and creeks came rushing down in mighty torrents carrying off the few bridges, so that it was almost impossible to travel far in any direction without "dug outs." Previous to this year, in 1850, we hear of the great

INDIAN WAR.

Through the month of May there had been some little trouble with Samuel Davison, a son of Mr. William Davison, and the Musquaquas. They being in close proximity, and the red men jealous of the encroachments of the whites upon their hunting grounds, a very respectable quarrel could be got up without much effort.

The Indians grew saucy and threatening, and going one day to Mr. John Campbell's claim, killed some of his hogs, drove off a few stock, and pointed their guns at him in a very wicked manner.

They had war dances, and were on the war path every day, armed and painted for a fight if there had been any more provocation. Twenty-four armed braves called at Mrs. Ralls' cabin one day, but seeing them coming she retreated to the bushes. A little nephew of hers took up an old hammer on his march and bravely made the declaration, that he could knock down "one big Ingin." But there was no harm done this time.

There is no doubt but that Davison burned corn belonging to the Indians, intending to exasperate them and have "a little brush," when the U. S. troops would expel the red men from Iowa. This was soon after the Mexican war, and the Indians were hardly settled into the belief that the Great Father at Washington was all powerful. The settlers on the south side of Iowa river united in a petition to Major Wood, of Fort Dodge, for help, who answered by saying, he could spare no troops then, and that they must remove from the vicinity, or protect themselves.

Among those who petitioned, and afterward went into the fort, were W. C. Smith, John Campbell, A. J. Smith, John Braddy, William and G. S. Ralls, Mr. Crowder, James L. Logan, Thomas and James Pearson, Blakely Brush, Joseph Cooper, Joseph M. Ferguson, S. Myers, Carpenter Geer, Thomas Sherman, William and Washington Asher, John Duck, Riley Majors, Thomas Sherman, —— Clifton, and Samuel Bowman.

Some tried to hire the Indians to leave. No! no, "heapy sick down in Missouri, all die — no go — lay bones in Iowa — heapy good!"

Hearing that there were at least 1,500 warriors getting ready for battle, these settlers we have mentioned, with their families, rendezvoused not far from a Mr. Robinson, with their stock, a few pigs and chickens, leaving the growing corn and gardens to the tender mercies of the Musquaquas. There was no attempt to raise wheat.

On arriving at Mr. Robinson's, they dispatched John Braddy and Mr. Greenbury Ralls after arms and ammunition; they commenced a stockade fort on Burke's Hill, where the remains are not to be seen at present. It was begun on the 11th of June, 1850, was occupied as soon as finished, and called Fort Robinson. In this, twenty-four families took refuge, leaving their crops, and made preparations for spending the summer in a close stockade, instead of going to Newport or the White Mountains.

The stockade was ninety feet square, built of puncheons, driven like piles into the ground, so that it made the fort walls about ten feet high. They brought in their furniture, bedding and provisions, but kept the cattle upon the outside. An occasional dog crept in; they heard the birds sing in the grove near by, and with over thirty children, there was no lack of music, even if the young calves fastened to the stockade were silent. The ladies patched their husbands' coats, and talked over the probabilities of an engagement with the redskins to keep from *ennui.* Their tents were made of wagon covers and old quilts; they had a few "chunk fires" in common; each family had their own table, with all they could get to eat upon it, so that after all there was plenty to do. Some of the meat was kept at Mr. Robinson's smoke house, also the milk and butter. William C. Smith (afterwards Judge) and John Campbell, generally went down to the Indians' camp every day, as a sort of outside guard and *detectives.* On the fifth day of the seige, they went again to the *Wickyups* and found them with large camp fires burning, and six kettles placed in a row, partly filled with water. Six good sized dogs were hung by the neck with strong twine, while the warriors danced around them for two hours, brandishing war clubs and looking war to the knife. After the perspiration had washed their faces of the paint, and they seemed pretty well exhausted, the squaws threw in the dogs into the kettles, where a sort of stew was made in the style of Macbeth's witches, with the exception it was all *dog*. After a little time this was dished out by the beldames, and given to the panting warriors, a little sugar being sprinkled on the savory morsel to make it more palatable.

There were about fifteen hundred braves assembled, and it looked dark for the little handful in the fort. The next day these gentlemen went again, and on the trail met four different parties of Indians well armed, who stopped them with their guns, and interrogated them as to the number of men in the fort. They answered, " big heap white men," and passed on, spending the night at Wm. Davison's. The seventh day the Indians came back again, and asked Captain James Logan, the commander of the fort, "how many guns?" He of course exaggerated the number of men and arms, and talked of a " big chief and Sioux," as Mr. Smith had done, when again they went away, sullen and still.

A very few days after this, Wm. Davison, thinking it would be a nice thing to test the courage of the garrison and commander, laid a plan for a sham attack. Letting the guard for the night (William Asher, who had a tremendous shot gun that had done some good execution among the wolves, Jack Braddy and Carpenter Geer,) into the secret, he went upon the hill where the cattle were lying down, when he raised a stampede. There was a hurrying of many feet; the cow-bells jingled at an awful rate, as if there were many warriors in the distance; reports of guns were heard, and the little company were soon fully aroused, and trying to meet the dreadful emergency.

Mrs. Logan sent to her husband, "keep your guns clean and your powder dry," as cool as if it were a shooting match for a Christmas turkey. Of course every light was extinguished; the Captain said, in hushed whispers, "Keep still and keep in your beds, women." Some of the little ones had quick ears, and it was very difficult to control *their* movements, but on the whole, they behaved well. There was of course a terrible excitement; the men grasped their guns, and some of the ladies commenced praying without preface, and others shouted, "Lord, save us." Poor old Mrs. Robinson, thinking she was not quite ready for the scalp knife, fell on her knees, repeating quite loud enough for a Musquaqua to hear had he listened, "Oh! Lord, I have tried to live in thy service through life, but I find I've not enough religion to die by. Give me more, Lord, please!"

Logan acted very well, and most of the men, but no Indians appeared over the walls, and finally about daylight, after finding no moccasin print, the garrison concluded they had been *sold*. Nothing could equal their chagrin and indignation, and had it not been that white men were scarce, somebody would have got a severe punishment.

One lady was *enciente*, the fright producing a dangerous illness, and no physician within fifty miles; matters looked dismal for the jokers who set the project on foot. But the lady recovered, and after quarreling some over the matter, it was concluded that the Indians did not mean trouble longer, so many of the families made preparations to leave. After about two weeks of suspense, they went back to their homes. Major Williams, of the U. S. Dragoons, finally received orders to remove the Musquaquas, and upon the appearance of a battalion of troops, the forest braves dropped their defiant manner, and peaceably withdrew, leaving the beautiful Iowa valley in this region to the plow and ax of the pioneer. Johnny Green and his few followers are the only representatives of this fighting stock. Johnny has the rheumatism, and boiled dog, be it ever so savory, can never give fire to his blood again, or strength to his palsied arm.

It is said by some after Logan told the Musquaquas that they were in the garrison for fear of the Sioux, they behaved more courteously, and showed the settlers how to make loop holes in the stockade for their guns. The Musquaquas certainly had more reason to fear their unforgiving enemies, the Sioux, than the peaceable whites, so that when Major Williams offered to make them presents, it was easy to make a negotiation, they believing that possibly there might be a coalition between the whites and Sioux.

There was another Indian scare in the neighborhood over the river in 1854, but it amounted to nothing. About this time commenced the county seat war, which we have delineated under the head of Marshalltown and Marietta. Next came the events connected with the Southern rebellion, which we have not space to particularize; and in 1862 the whisky troubles arose, when a mob seized whisky that was in the hands of the sheriff, and emptied it on the ground. As the vile stuff was stored at Mr. Harvey Beckwith's, in Marshalltown, and his wife sick at the time, the excitement caused her a great deal of unnecessary suffering. Mr. Beckwith, being a law and order man, was bound to protect the property in the absence of the sheriff, and the persons connected with the affair should have waited and acted with more care and discrimination, although if ever there is justification for a mob, it is in spilling the accursed stuff wherever found, and as soon as possible. In looking over the different townships the reader will learn of the particulars connected with the history of Marshall county further.

LE GRAND

Township is the pioneer settlement of the county, Mr. Joseph Davison having come in 1847, and settled upon one of the hills east of the Iowa river, in a beautiful grove, which still bears his name. Here he lived in a little cabin with the Indians, without a white neighbor for fifty miles. His brother came a little later, Mr. William Davison, and in a short time they both had good farms and supplied new comers with the necessaries of life, before there were a half dozen families in Marshall to till the soil.

This township has grove and open prairie and the very best stone for building purposes and other uses, in the State. Davison being well aware of its advantages, alternately threatened and coaxed the Indians, until there were enough whites in the country to stand up in bold front and drive them from their hunting grounds.

The Davisons were kind neighbors, but they removed to Oregon a few years ago "to find elbow room." Jostled there by brawny arms, they will probably turn up in Sitka with a pole bedstead and a wooden spoon, until civilization shall send them under the lee of the north pole.

Mr. S. N. Knode came to Le Grand in February of 1852, and finding a hut that had been used by a passing hunter, without door or chimney, or even a floor, moved his family soon after into this abode and began life in Iowa. For a few weeks, the smoke found its way out from the fire-place through the logs, (no "chinkin" to impede its progress,) and other families coming in, there were in this little cabin of sixteen feet square, thirty-six persons, counting the children, who found a home.

The Allmans, Voorhees, and Webbs, lived with them till they could prepare a home for themselves.

And to add to this large family, travelers had to be entertained, and one night, four more were added to the original thirty-six, making it a matter of serious moment where to sandwich the crowd, so that each could have a puncheon for a bed. The "Judge" as he is familiarly called, once owned an immense tract of land, but through a relative, became involved, and was obliged to sell at a great sacrifice. As he is reported to be an heir to the famous Knode estate in Holland, we have no doubt that testy old Dame Fortune has a card yet in store for him.

Messrs. Jehu and James Allman came here in the same spring, and had cabins built on the site of Le Grand village in the north part of town. They have been prominent men here, and done all they could to make this a business point. Mr. JAMES ALLMAN and M. Webb were the first to lay out Le Grand village in 1852. Mr. Sanders of Iowa City, was called to survey out Lafayette, and on his homeward journey did a like service for the aforesaid, which occupies a very pleasant location south of the Iowa river. Had the Cedar Rapids Railroad Company done itself and the village justice, Le Grand would have been a formidable rival to pretentious towns on the line; but Blair's cupidity in attempting to plant a town two miles from nowhere, did not succeed, and a solitary hotel with a rickety old station-house which is a disgrace to any corporation, is all that remains of Blair's embryo city. The Railroad Company must have been to much more expense in going around so far, that Le Grand might be left out in the cold ; and what is more aggravating, the citizens had petted them in every possible manner, entertaining their officers and agents to the best in the town, and then gave them $12,000 in subscriptions, which was coolly pocketed without a thankee, and the smoke of their locomotives wreathes around the hills two miles distant, when they could have had the depot within forty rods, with less cost, and helped build up the town of their benefactors. It is said that prominent citizens of Marshalltown helped the nefarious scheme of John A. Blair, so as to kill off Le Grand, in revenge against those who voted for Marietta through the war. Mr. James Allman had the opinion that Le Grand would finally get a slice of Tama county and another from Grundy and Marshall, and become a county seat. Marietta being the farthest away, was less dangerous than Marshalltown, so he was quite inimical at times, against the latter place ; but finally "Cobtown," as her enemies called her, gave a decision in favor of Marshalltown, and was loyal thereafter, with the exception of thirteen voters.

Among the early settlers we have already mentioned, was Mr. Robert Voorhees, who is still a citizen and an excellent man ; also, Mr. Rollin Richards came about the same time ; Mr. Ami Willets came a little later— is a Friend, and lives on the Davison farm. He is quite wealthy, and is well known for his charities, that are so characteristic of the beautiful religion of George Fox. Mr. Israel Willets is also an early settler, and living on a highly cultivated farm ; is wealthy, and much respected. Mr. Hiram Hammond came in 1854, and has been connected with mills, in the stock and grain business, has a large dry goods store, and is one of those pleasant, quiet men, who would make friends anywhere.

In 1853 there was a county election held at Griffith's mill in this township, where W. C. Smith was whig competitor against Griffith, democratic, for the office of county judge. There were twenty-two voters, and the result was in favor of Smith, although Griffith was so sure of election that he built a cabin at Marietta, with the expectation of occupying it. This was the first whig victory of the county. Mr. James Allman was the first postmaster, and in getting his commission, found this ambitious Mr. Griffith in the lists against him.

But Mr. A. was indorsed in Iowa City by democratic patronage, and he was appointed to the office. Mr. Griffith was so chagrined at this result and that of the other contest, that he sold out and left the country. Previous to this, there was no postoffice short of Marengo, forty-five miles distant.

Chesley Coppic, a distant relative of Coppic, the co-laborer of John Brown, was the first justice, and Dr. Young, since deceased, practicing physician. Riley McCool came here in 1856, and had quite a large stock of dry goods, but there came an unlucky fire and burned store and contents to the ground. Mr. McCool has been engaged since in the stock business, buying cattle for the Chicago markets, and handles a large amount of money; also, Hammond Brothers ship stock in large quantities to the same yards.

WOMEN'S RIGHTS.

In the summer of 1856, a saloon was opened by some vile wretch, and after vending his wicked wares for a time, the ladies concluded to try force, to stop it, as pleasant words had been exhausted. A party of nine ladies entered the doggery and while some were engaged in knocking in the barrels with axes, etc., Mrs. Jack Wheitzell threw out brandy bottles, tumblers, etc., then taking the keeper by the nape of the neck sent him kiting out of the door after them. The whole concern was demolished, and it was the last one of the kind that ever lifted its brazen front in the village. Mrs. Hiram Hammond reports that she "made very awkward work in handling the ax on the barrel heads." They were all arrested, and taking venue, they were brought before Justice Yeamans of Marshalltown, who had them in court three days, but through some flaw in the indictment, they were released. The next day, Samuel Hoffman, the bachelor constable, might be seen on the search for the immortal nine,

to bring them to justice yet again. Some had gone to
Tama on a visit, others were out of sight, in the cellar
and in the stables, and it is said, Hoffman swore it
was the hardest day's work he ever did, trying to
capture the girls.   Finally, it fell through by default,
and the women were victorious, upheld too, by an
overwhelming public sentiment.

They have a Good Templars' lodge of one hundred
members.   The Friends have a pretty brick church,
seventy by sixty feet, with two hundred names on its
records, that subscribe to their self-denying principles.
They were forward in assisting the freedmen, and give
many beautiful examples of christian benevolence.
They have several lady preachers among them; we
might mention Mrs. Julia McCool, a lady of many
pleasant social qualities, as well as gifts of pulpit
teaching.

Mrs. Jonathan Reed, the President of the Soldiers
Aid Society, who wrought many months unweariedly,
is a member of the Methodist Episcopal Church, and
will receive further notice under the head of Greencastle.

Mr. Ed. Lockwood, now of Marshaltown, and sheriff
of the county in 1859, after a very spirited contest,
once lived here.   He and his worthy lady are too well
known for us to add anything to their beautiful life
record.

A very excellent citizen of Le Grand is Mr. S. Good-
rich, the owner of the magnificent stone quarry, which,
for building purposes, cannot be equaled in the State.

LE GRAND INSTITUTE,

That had the late much lamented Professor James
Guthrie, from Antioch College, Ohio, as its presiding
officer, is an honor to the village and county—has a
fine brick structure forty by sixty feet, which will cost
when finished, $10,000.   Has a senior class of thirty-

five, and will in time become of great benefit to Iowa. Le Grand has certainly made a good beginning, for, as far as it is finished, the building and furniture is of the most substantial character.

It is under the immediate care of the Christians or New Lights, who are a peculiar people, having some singular ceremonies, yet, no doubt, do a great deal of good in the village. Any sect that helps to elevate humanity and lead man back to his Maker, should be encouraged. They have a membership of, perhaps, one hundred and fifty, and exercise a great influence in this community.

There is also a little Methodist Episcopal church under the pastoral care of Revs. Ward and Hayman, that is increasing in numbers and influence. They talk of building a chapel this season, which consummation is most devoutly to be wished, as it will accommodate both church and sabbath school.

PRESENT PROSPERITY.

Le Grand contains about four hundred inhabitants, has splendid mills which we hear of in every direction, Rock Valley mills and Le Grand; also three dry goods stores, Jehu Allman & Co., Hammond Bros., and John Mote & Co. It has, too, one hardware store, two drug, and one boot and shoe store, furniture shops, two hotels, two millinery shops, one grocery, and one large harness shop. The stores all do a good business; Hammond & Brothers buying stock and grain to a large extent, and have the express agency also. Mr. J. W. Allman is postmaster, and in Dr. Whipple and Dr. Smith, the inhabitants have every confidence. There are several clergymen, and a Mrs. Samuel Coates, wife of a wealthy, prominent citizen, is also a powerful preacher of the Christian denomination.

If the Railroad Company will come to their senses, and build a depot at the McCool crossing, we shall bespeak a promising future for this sprightly, enterprising town.

TIMBER CREEK,

The next township by order of settlement, was named after the beautiful stream of water that courses through its whole domain, bestowing the immense advantages of never-failing water, forest, and a beauty of landscape rivaling the parks of old England— such lofty trees are here, as if set out by the hand of some cunning gardener. There are signs of coal along its bluffs, of great benefit to the county, if capital would but seek out the hidden treasures.

Mr. J. M. Ferguson and Josiah Cooper settled on the south side of the grove in 1848. Mr. Ferguson lived here a good many years, became quite wealthy, and removed to Albion. Mr. F. had the usual cabin, built without nails, stick chimney and dirt floor, for a time, as there were no settlements this side of Oskaloosa or Iowa City, and but three or four families on the route.

His brother, George Ferguson, lived here some time, then removed to Le Grand, where he owned one of the best farms in the State. His horses have been justly admired at our County Fairs, and he lately sold a premium stallion to Mr. Jerolman, of Eden, for nine hundred dollars. Mr. Ferguson has recently sold his farm to Judge Van Shaack, of New York, and lives near Marshalltown.

Mr. William Asher lived here awhile, and built, in the corner of Le Grand township, the first grist mill in the county. It was a very rude affair and only cracked kernels of corn a little, and did not attempt flour. But this was much better than to crack it between two stones about the size of a half bushel, then be obliged to eat the grit and dirt which necessarily came with the attrition process of the rude machine.

Mr. Asher was a very good man, but soon after this he froze his left foot, and amputation being necessary, he could not survive the shock and died in the operation.

Carpenter Geer, another of the garrison at Fort Robinson, built the first saw mill in the county, and these enterprises fell into the hands of Mr. Griffith, who kept them operating for a time, but after turning his attention to politics, sold out to Mr. Brinnock and all went into the hands of Isaacher Scholfield, afterwards the best mills in the State.

John Campbell came to the northwestern part of the township in 1849, a young man from Linn county, and having pleasant memories of the place, gave the name also to Linn Creek. He had a good farm, ready to supply with provisions the citizens of Marshalltown, ere Anson had it scarcely christened.

W. C. Smith, and his brother, Jackson Smith, came in March, 1848. Mr. W. C. Smith was acting county clerk in early times, was judge four years, and has been a teacher, of an excellent character, in Timber Creek. He has ecclesiastical license to preach in the Christian church, and fills the pulpit with great ability, we are told. As his history is identified with the county, we shall speak further of Judge Smith on another page.

Mr. Jackson Smith has a splendid farm in this township—was the first justice in the county, and married the first couple that ever placed their necks in the yoke matrimonial, within its limits. The names of the happy pair were Mr. Almerian Geer, son of Carpenter Geer, and Miss Ballard, daughter of Philip Ballard, of Iowa township. This was in the spring of 1850, and Mr. Smith reports that it was one of the pleasantest times in the whole cycle of pioneer hilarity. They had a good supper, danced, and joked the girls, tucked the bride into her snowy bed-drapery, and laughed at her discomfiture.

4

Mr. Greenbury S. Ralls, brother of William Ralls, lived in Marshall near the edge of Timber Creek township. He bore severe privations bravely, and early filled many of the minor offices of this section with trust, and is in every way a kind neighbor and citizen. He now lives in Iowa township.

Another one of the rank and file of Logan's men (who, by the way, was himself a Timber Creek citizen, and since deceased), was Mr. Riley Majors, who lives very near the corner of Jefferson, having entered his claim of over two hundred acres. We believe he owned some lots in New Jefferson, a town that once was staked off on Jackson Smith's farm. There were several cabins built, and its lots were talked of once among land agents and real estate brokers in Marshall county.

Mr. Henry Burke who lives on the old Robinson claim, near the remains (if any) of the stockade fort, came here in 1853 from Southern Illinois. He raised a large family of sons and daughters; his wife died some years since, very much sorrowed after by the relatives and neighbors. One of his daughters married Solomon Miller, Esq., of Marshalltown, who left a splendid army record, and is now one of the most prominent citizens of the city. He has literary talent, and would fill an important position in county affairs, if our people will remember the soldiers in future.

Mr. Burke has one of the best cultivated farms in the county, over two hundred acres of growing crops, with a lovely fruit and walnut orchard back of his farm-house; sheep, cattle, etc.; and Mr. B. came here comparatively poor. He is brother-in-law to Mr. Powers, and also to Mr. Turner, once a citizen of this section, now in Missouri.

Mr. Crowder and Mr. Meyers, now of Iowa township, were neighbors on Timber creek, and the old settlers used to meet every week, and had parties, where all came, and eat pounded or cracked corn, with many a joke as to the power of each other's teeth in crushing the substitute for bread.

At one time, Mr. Greer went to Jack Braddy's, a *near* neighbor, who lived seven or eight miles away, which was a mere *bagatelle* as to distance. Being a widower, he wished to pay his addresses to a young lady there. Taking Jack by the ear, he whispers very softly, " Do you think she will *set ?* " meaning, that if she would *set* with him it was equivalent to an affirmative answer to his suit.

They had a quilting at Mr. Robinson's, the gentlemen being invited with the ladies; the dinner-pot with its savory ham was boiled out of doors over a chunk fire ; guests, excepting the quilters, sat on the wood-pile and rude seats outside, so as to make room for those who wrought by the long ungainly frames. Corn-bread, good coffee, wild fruit, with the delicious ham, was the *cuisine* on the occasion. After supper came the height of enjoyment, to shake the quilt over the prettiest girl ; who blushed scarlet, and is now a happy wife, and mother of seven boys.

The Sherwoods came in 1856, and have good farms, also Mr. Asahel Stone, near Washington, whose splendid dairy is so identified with his name that he is familiarly termed the " cheese man." He brought considerable capital from the East, and buying a large number of cows, started the enterprise of supplying Duchess County butter and cheese for Marshall. And it is quite equal to that noted brand in the Eastern market, and we commend others, who attempt to palm off their white oak imitations on the public, to visit his establishment and take lessons of the gentleman farmer, Asahel Stone.

Mr. Forey, the father-in-law of the genial Dr. Rickey, of Marshalltown, is also a citizen of Timber Creek. He has lived here eight years, was loyal and true, when others were very conservative and wore butternut emblems. His son, David Forey, served with bravery in the " old Thirteenth Iowa."

Messrs. Owen, Blackburn, and Monahon, of Kentucky, came here quite recently, have good farms and also have made splendid improvements in the short time which they·have been engaged in the work. Mrs. Monahan is a pleasant hostess and entertains the *creme le creme* of Marshalltown aristocracy with old fashioned Kentucky welcome.

In the north edge of the township, lives Father Gourley, a member of the M. E. Church for many years, and a worthy disciple of Wesley he is, too. He came to Timber Creek in 1854, has a good farm under cultivation, and is able and willing to help all those in need.

We close with a hasty mention of Mr. Hildebrand who was an early settler, Mr. Cooper, and Mr. Rogers, the energetic farmer living near the Marshall line, who has been here since 1857. He sent a brave boy to the Union Army, who died there, without a comrade near him.

This township is one of the best in the county, with good school houses, plenty of timber, mills, etc.

MARIETTA

Township is situated west of Marshall ; the Iowa river and the Little Minerva, with their tributaries, water its surface, and " the lay of the land " is very fine, especially in the southern part. In early times this township had the advantage of the county seat, had county roads centralizing at the village, and much of the western travel to the Plains passed through, giving a market to the surplus products of the soil. Common highways or turnpikes, used to be quite a help, but the towns in Iowa now build on the railroad lines, and the common roads crook around the fields to get to them.

Doctor Bush was the first settler in Marietta, near the corner of Iowa township on the Iowa river. This was in 1850. He practiced some, but hunted more, as there were only a half dozen families to take pills, and game was plenty.

A Mr. Peterman was the next to swing an ax. He came the same year, and pounded corn for bread, drove off ravenous wolves from his door, and had quite a good supply of provisions to sell, after his farm was opened up to the new comers. He has removed from Marietta.

Mr. William Dishon came from Oskaloosa in 1851, and soon after brought the first stock of goods into the county, settling near the river just north of the present town and commenced business, intending to lay out something of a village there, but others coming in, he was persuaded by Judge Hobbs to move into Marietta. He was the first village postmaster. Mahlon Collins followed, with another stock of Yankee notions, and afterward was a prominent man in the county seat war as well as Mr. Dishon.

There was a merchant by the name of Darlington who sold quite a large lot of goods on credit, whose daughter, Eudora, was the first white child born here.

Quite a number of Hicksites and orthodox Quakers came into Marietta; they were men of unflinching integrity and gave a high tone to public sentiment. Among these, was Doctor Hixon, who at least had *some* Quaker blood in his veins, and lived near the corner of Iowa township. He built the first mill on the Little Minerva. He will be remembered as representing the county in the lower house of the Legislature in 1863-4. The doctor is a temperance man and has been in many a good work for the people's welfare.

How bright the name of Lot Holmes shines on the Marietta record! He was a native of Loudon county,

Va., but becoming early convinced of the sin of slavery, would not vote or live in the Old Dominion. He was connected with the Underground Railroad in Salem, Ohio, and has always been in the conflict, taking stand with Garrison and Phillips of the old Anti-Slavery Guard.

He and his noble wife have been among the first to organize societies for the help of the soldiers and freedmen. They have spent, with others, a good deal of time and money to get fugitives through from Missouri to the North Star. We mention, that he bought a wig at one time, in Chicago, for a black boy's disguise, paying fifteen dollars for it. Associated with him in all the benevolent enterprises of the day, was Mr. Stacey Nichols, also a Friend, and like Mr. Holmes uses the plain language.

Mr. William Marsh, living on the hill south of Marietta, a father-in-law of Mr. Abram Stanley, of Albion, is also an early settler, and the same sweet charities characterize him as they do others of that noble church, the Friends. Also Mr. Lackey, whose "Pink" knew how to use a shot-gun in the Marietta war; and Mr. John Amos, who suffered with a terrible cancer many years. He was one of the early county commissioners, and he is remembered, by Mr. Henry Green and others, to have said in the above-mentioned war, "Let me to the front; I have but a few months to live with this cancer, and I'll sell my life as dearly as possible among the rascals."

Doctor WHEALEN came to Marietta in October, 1853, being the first physician, with the exception of some inebriated quack, who left that season. The summer and fall were quite unhealthy, many were discouraged, but the appearance of a good physician was hailed with delight. Doctor Whealen practiced all through Marshall and even into the adjoining counties; on horseback, over sloughs without bridges, perhaps take a canoe and cross the Iowa at night; and in the cabins of the poor emigrants, saw sights to make a sensitive man sick of the profession. The emigration was heavy that year, and the farmers in this section could not supply all who came, with provisions, and especially milk and butter. The cows not being properly cared for, it was impossible to obtain these necessaries. The doctor's family had no milk or butter for months. Mrs. Whealen wrote to a friend in Ohio, that cows did not give milk in Iowa, for she had " tried all belonging to the neighbors and they were dry."

The doctor made the most of their furniture— three-legged stools, splint-bottomed chairs, a cradle made of a shoe box, and a dry goods box for a *beaufet.* What Iowa housekeeper of the early day knew not how to arrange this cupboard so as to get in all the dishes, with a corner for a bottle of hair oil and the fine tooth comb! Mrs. Whealen managed to entertain twenty-two persons in her cabin for awhile, but at night the cradle, chairs, and table were set out of doors to be occupied by ghosts of departed Musquaquas—covering the entire floor with beds, sometimes pinning overcoats and dresses together for a partition to shade the young girls' sweet faces. She, that ruled her spirit, was greater than one who takes a city, in such times.

Mr. Delos Arnold taught the first school in the old court house, and his neighbors remember the epoch by his writing letters for the Eastern papers in the rookery.

Alexander Crow kept the first hotel, dividing the honors of Boniface with A. L. Hall, now of Marshall-town, and a Mr. Shively.

The Williams family came about this time, perhaps some later, with small means, but now, as a family, have as much influence and what is called " position," as any in the county. Four daughters and two sons— the mother may well be proud of their success in life.

Doctor Waters, also, was well liked in Marietta, having a large and lucrative practice. Mr. James Geitzcy started a cabinet shop, some years after, thus displacing the rustic furniture of the above-mentioned patentee, Dr. Whealen. He now lives in Marshalltown. W. C. Smith, also Mr. Woodward, and other officers, came here to live after the county seat was located.

Through the township there were a few families scattered about, trying to live in their little cabins. A Mr. Braddock, east of the present village of Marietta, who now has a beautiful house, was one of these. Also Mr. Coddington, Mr. Kimberly, and others.

Mr. D. Moninger, a citizen here, pays the heaviest tax of any man in the county.

The commissioners from the Iowa Legislature appointed in 1850-1, traveled over Marshall in every direction to locate the county-seat, and after passing some very eligible points, selected

MARIETTA,

Which is situated nearly in the geographical center of the county, about one-half mile from the Iowa river, and six miles north-east from Marshalltown. The town site was surveyed by Messrs. Hobbs and Dawson, October 11, 1851, and the capital located there without demur, except from Anson. Afterwards an addition was made to the corporation by Messrs. Boardman and Leaming. It is built on bottom land, with heavy timber north, and bluffs southward, and except in very wet weather, the town presents a pleasing appearance, and had it not been for some natural advantages of Marshalltown, and the obstinate pertinacity of some of its citizens, Marietta, like Marengo, might have been a county seat, and quite a city, after all. Its lots at one time brought a good figure, and many an owner of its corners, deplored the "war," as a losing thing for investments, especially if he was speculating upon borrowed capital, as many did before the crash of 1857.

The contest commenced about the year 1853 between the rival towns, and every artifice and device was used on both sides to control votes, so as to gain the desired end. The most bitter hatred was engendered for a time, and the most insulting invectives were indulged in without measure. As a specimen of the ridicule used to control public sentiment, we quote from the files of the Iowa Central Journal, the organ for Marshalltown : " A Frenchman lately from Paris, is negotiating for the purchase of the public square in Marietta to raise frogs for that market ! " It may be, some believed the romance.

On another occasion, a gentleman by the name of Crookham, an extensive property holder in Marietta, was down to Marshalltown on business; it was arranged by a few of the sharp ones of the latter place, to badger the poor man a little, so calling some stranger (to Crookham) among a group of themselves, with a great deal of horror and uplifted hands, they told him, in his hearing, that a man was actually drowned in the public square of Marietta only the week before ! Nothing could equal the representative's rage at such abominable falsehoods of his much-abused town, and he went home swearing about Marshalltown, where they told such awful whoppers.

The organ for Marietta was known among the newspapers as The Marietta Express. It was published by T. High and A. J. Kenney. It had no reputed editor at first, although its leaders were supposed to have been written by Hon. H. E. J. Boardman. At this time in the history of our county, if report was true, he wielded a powerful pen against the claims of Marshalltown to public favor. The Express accused its citizens of bribery, fraud, and other evil things, and alludes to the Iowa Central as a *"smut machine,"* a "dried up pump," etc. These things called out a rejoinder from the aforesaid, and so the contest went on, till finally this newspaper war began to be very sensibly shown in public sentiment.

Besides Marshalltown, Marietta had a rival in La-fayette, now called Albion, and in this triangular fight, the Marietta Express had to keep its eyes well open to watch all the corners. Albion could not hope to have the county-seat, but by killing off Marietta, she might build up her rival, and in course of time would get a sop for herself, of some public institution, the High School, or some seminary of learning. The Marietta Express fought bravely and well, but when the county seat was removed to Marshalltown, it was obliged to succumb, and died an honorable death.

But we will go back to a period earlier than the Express,—when Mr. Woodward was treasurer of the county, and the business so light that he carried the blank receipts in his hat. Mr. Weatherly relates, that his tax receipt ran in this style : " This certifies that W. Weatherly has paid his taxes for the year of 1852," without saying anything about the property, etc. We think it would puzzle Mr. Gerhart to carry on business in this fashion.

After Judge Hobbs' term of office had expired, there must necessarily be a new election. Mr. W. C. Smith failing to get his bonds in some manner, correct, after a successful canvass, Esquire Atwater, being prosecuting attorney, was *de facto* judge, and wishing to retain the judicial mantle, was opposed to Mr. Smith's holding the office, and ordered another election. The Marshalltown interest supported Mr. Thomas Griffith, and Marietta, to burlesque the whole affair, supported a Mrs. Durbin. The result was, on the official count, that the lady had five majority ! *Le premier victorie!* for woman's rights. She was bought off with the present of a new dress, and Judge Smith appointed in her stead. To this last item we affix the date of 1853.

Speaking of judges, reminds us of a little scene that occurred here while McFarland was on the bench. A young lawyer from Burlington by the name of Wood, was facetiously termed by the profession, "Old Timber." At this court he was in the midst of a fine rhetorical display in submitting his case to the jury, when the head of an immense donkey thrust itself through the window and interrupted the eloquent lawyer with an outrageous braying. McFarland cries out, "Hold up, Old Timber, this honorable court cannot entertain both of your opinions on this question at the same time!" Nothing could equal the intense satisfaction of court, lawyers and audience, with the exception of Mr. Wood, who was terribly chagrined, and to crown all, lost his case.

Another swing of memory's bells and we hear of the Grand Coop of the Oriental Order of Bachelors, who assembled sometimes in an office, occasionally in a kitchen. A Mr. McKye was Chief Mogul, Jefferson Crookham, Thomas Mercer, Mr. Plug, Mr. Willow, and we have no doubt, Mr. D. L. Arnold, were members. It seemed they were a jolly set of fellows, but lacked success among the ladies through timidity. The affair was so ridiculous in a Western community, that the Marietta girls took pity on the whole caboose and married them, in due time. The High Mogul was the first to succumb, and made a very good husband in spite of the bad discipline in the Coop.

Marietta had a Literary Society whose wits weekly shone like stars, in the old court house. Many questions were discussed, essays read, and all served to keep the little village from stagnation. One evening, an infidel sentiment was promulgated by a lady, but the pitiful atheist was soon consigned to disgrace. There were quite a number of these weak persons in

the neighborhood, but happily they have seen their
folly, and there is now scarcely one to be found.

About this time, in the winter of 1855–6, there was
quite an excitement about the Fulton Air Line Railroad that was to make Marietta a point on its route to
the Missouri. The county-seat war was still carried
on, and notwithstanding the cloud that arose in the
eastern horizon over Marshalltown, not bigger than
a man's hand, everything went merry as a marriage-
bell. The town received quite an accession to its
population in the year 1856, as did the State generally,
and there was a good deal of business done in land
agencies.

One of the most successful lawyers at the time,
was Hon. H. E. J. BOARDMAN, who was always ready
to work for the interest of Marietta. Hon. D. L.
Arnold was also practicing law, and in the real estate
business.

Everything was done to control the election that
was to come off in April of this year, and upon
the trial, it went in favor of Marietta. The citizens
quietly took a nap over this, thinking this was a
quietus, but their vigilant foe was stealing the hearts
of the people by many devices. One potent reason
given against Marietta was, that the Fulton Railroad
would never be built, and that Marietta might always
remain in the swamp without an outlet, excepting the
Iowa river ; but letters were published and all assur-
ances made, that the railroad would be built. Beside
presents that were freely distributed by Marshalltown
to control votes, the Town Hall was finished and ready
for the occupancy of the District Court—and no taxa-
tion. This, in the hard times of 1857–8, had influence
on the farmers of the county. Marshalltown had an
accession of energy and capital as well as Marietta,
and her pertinacious, prominent men were determined
on making it the county seat. A solemn pledge was
made, that as long as life lasted there should never

be any giving up of the contest, and that they would not tolerate a traitor in the midst of Marshalltown, or allow any one inimical to their interests to hold any office there.

With these drawbacks, when Marietta came into the field at the spring election of 1858, victory perched upon the banners of her rival. When the reports came in, Wells Rice and a few others went up to Marietta to feel of her pulse. There was no excitement and they seemed to take it coolly. It soon became apparent that they, likewise, had written upon their escutcheon, *nil desperandum*. Knowing, that in a new community there always is some informality, she was ready to throw out the votes of Marion, Le Grand and Greencastle. Their returns were not dated, neither were they certified to by the proper officers ; so that legitimately she had a right to contest the election on the letter of the law, though she was well aware that the majority was now in favor of her antagonist. Judge Smith declared in favor of Marietta, or rather the board of county canvassers had so decided previous to his action. An alternative writ of mandamus was then issued by order of the District Court, Judge Thompson presiding, on the first day of the April term, commanding the county judge to take to his assistance two justices of the county, re-canvass the returns, including the three rejected townships, and declare the result accordingly, or show cause why he should not do so, on or before the third day of the term. The counsel for Marietta was the Hon. Enoch Eastman.

Judge Smith filed exceptions, and refusing to answer or re-canvass, another writ was issued against him, peremptorily ordering him to re-canvass, but this he disobeyed, and appealed to the Supreme Court, where it was argued at the June term, 1858. In the following December term of the Supreme Court the case came up again. William Penn Clark, of Iowa

City, counsel for Marshalltown, and Hon. C. C. Cole for Marietta, and the judgment of the District Court was affirmed. In the early part of January, 1850, the clerk of the Supreme Court issued a peremptory writ of mandamus ordering Judge Smith, with the other officers of the board of canvassers, to re-canvass. The justices, thinking of the money invested in Marietta, thinking of their homes and ambitions, decided against counting in the rejected townships, but Judge Smith, under advice of shrewd council from Desmoines, declared in favor of them; for the law plainly says that there shall be no disfranchisement, except in cases of fraud. But the decision of a majority of the *jurat* was in favor of Marietta, and it was thus rendered. Meantime, under certain representations, a writ of injunction was procured from Judge Thompson, restraining the county judge from removing the records from Marietta, this writ being held in reserve. These proceedings so exasperated the people of Marshalltown, that they filed information against Judge Smith and Justices Turner and Wallahan for dereliction of duty, and they were brought down to Marshalltown for trial before Justice Yeaman. On a writ of habeas corpus being issued by the county clerk, J. L. Williams acting as judge, Messrs. Turner and Wallahan were released, but Judge Smith was still held in durance vile. William T. Hepburn was prosecuting attorney in the case, H. C. Henderson, assistant counsel, and H. E. J. Boardman for the defense.

Pending this trial there was a great deal of excitement at Marshalltown, and the last evening of the proceedings, in a speech made by Boardman, he intimated that Henderson had told an untruth. Of course this exasperated the counsel to fever heat; he drew up to Boardman, cane in hand, demanding a retraction. There were a few Marietta men in the room, who rather huddled together about their champion. Some one at the door cried out, "Blow out the lights, Lynch the Marietta rascals!" Some of the candles disappeared, but there were enough left to show Boardman in the tableaux, pale, yet cool as a cucumber, and waving his right hand with a tragic look that Forrest might wear in Coriolanus—"Gentlemen, you can impose upon Marietta and her rights now, but you will feel different when the cold steel of a hundred bayonets is running through your hearts." This hifalutin and his coolness, seemed to have some effect, for Henderson left the room in a few minutes, and the crowd below stairs began to cry out for Judge Smith. Frightened, as perhaps hundreds of others might have been, already badgered by months of anxiety with the most ferocious of the Marietta men, (for this excitement had got beyond the control of all peaceable persons,) Judge Smith, as a Mason, demanded the protection of the craft, in the persons of Mr. Woodbury and Dr. Glick. They escorted him through the crowd and he went first to Mr. Woodbury's, when he expressed a wish to go to his father's. They accompanied him there and left him with no person about the house but the family. In the course of the night, Mr. Babcock, the Methodist clergyman, went to Marietta for Mrs. Smith, taking Mr. Woodbury's carriage, but she refused to come, influenced by the Marietta ladies. At the house there, Mr. Babcock was made to fall into a trap through a hole in the floor, with an oilcloth cover carefully placed over it. But he came back to Marshalltown about three o'clock in the morning, and, calling on Judge Smith, reported matters unsuccessful in that direction. Mr. B. then advised Judge Smith to go home with him and take some rest, as he seemed so fatigued with watching, intimating there were persons in the yard. It is said that Marietta had men watching him to see that he did no mischief to her interests; as well as Marshalltown had a guard at the bridge. It is impossible to know how many, if any, irresponsible persons were in the vicinity. Mr.

Woodbury and Dr. Glick both say, that none was sent
from headquarters.

It is said by a responsible man, that when Judge
Smith declared he would not issue a proclamation for
a special election in favor of giving Albion the swamp
lands without a petition from two-thirds of the voters,
that he was surrounded by leading men from Marietta
and told that he *must* do it, or he would be sorry, etc.
Cowed down, the Judge burst into tears and said he
would sell his house and lot for half price and leave
Marietta.

We only give facts, and do not say that Marietta
had a man on the ground. He was no doubt consci-
entious in all his acts, his enemies cannot say he received a bribe, but he was too easily intimidated.
A copperhead on Timber Creek, once frightened him
in a terrible manner with words.

About seven o'clock, on the morning of the eleventh
of January, 1859, Judge Smith is found in a chamber
at Mr. Babcock's, with a sheet of paper before him with
the county seal, or rather an impression, upon it, and
several prominent men of Marshalltown as witnesses
to a re-canvass of the vote upon the county seat, and
an order for the removal of the records. Judge Smith,
astonished to find the county seal, issued an order,
although J. L. Williams, acting as county judge, would
have been the proper officer. Judge Smith after signing this order, was released informally, we believe.
It was reported that Mr. Woodbury obtained the impression in the following manner : Being at the court
house in Marietta to convey a deed to some person, he
asked the judge if he could have a sheet of paper.
Upon its presentation, while the judge was busily engaged, he carelessly let the county seal fall upon the
paper, then folding it up with others, it was ready for
use when the proper time came, and was presented to
Judge Smith.

Another little piece of *finesse* we notice, to show

the care that was used lest there should be an advantage gained by Marietta. When the returns were made out from Marshall township, the signing of the jurat was neglected by the proper officers, at the spring election of 1858. A few found this out, and with a secret pledge that it should not be divulged, they proceeded to rectify the mistake. Old Mr. Rice and Father Dunton started off in the night, and going to Judge Smith got the poll-book and brought it back to Marshalltown and made it correct, without the knowledge of another person in Marietta.

This is no hap-hazard revelation, and could it have been found out by Marietta, a day or two later, it would have made Marshall as famous for mistakes as the rejected three townships from the east side.

After Judge Smith had given the order to remove the records from Marietta, messengers were sent in every direction, to the friends of Marshalltown. For several nights the Town Hall in that place had been watched by zealous citizens for fear that some incendiary from the rival village might reduce the hard earned structure to ashes. The whole town was on the alert, and as the morning dawned cold and frosty, it ushered in the memorable day of the eleventh of January, 1859, and the

MARIETTA BATTLE.

Sheriff Harris ordered out the Bowen Guards, a militia company whose prowess had extended over land and sea, as a *posse comitatus*, to take, have, and to hold the capital of Marshall county. Their leader buckled on a sword that had never been wet in human gore, the men made hurried preparations for the attack, and every warlike weapon which could be found in the village was hunted up and scoured by the best of cotton rags and elbow grease, beside their own regular arms.

5

Early in the morning, wagons came into town filled with armed men, orderlies were flying about carrying despatches, and everything denoted " war to the knife." Messrs. Boardman and Turner started out before the Guards were quite ready, and stopped at Mr. Joseph Allen's, but were delayed by their carriage breaking down—the tire coming off. But whipping up, they concluded to go on without any tire, and in danger of going into general bankruptcy of wheel and buggy, they rushed into Marietta to make preparations for defense. But we will glance backward to the irate town on Linn Creek.

Sheriff L. L. Harris is making himself very conspicuous in going through military exercises, and we will insert his order, for he denied ever giving any to Captain Shurtz, when he feared damages from Marietta people, as rumored. The order ran thus :

MARSHALL, Jan. 11, 1859.

Capt. E. SHURTZ, Esq.:

Sir—You are hereby commanded to summon your Company to be and appear before the Court House in Marietta, in Marshall county, Iowa, armed and equipped as by law required, forthwith—and by no means whatsoever harm or molest any one without my orders. Hereof fail not, under the pains and penalties of the laws of the State of Iowa.

You are further commanded to strictly forbid any loose talk or swearing, or even threats from any one of your Company.　　　　　L. L. HARRIS,
Sheriff Marshall County, Iowa.

Herein lay the delegated powers of the Bowen Guards, *et literatim.*

There was a large corps of observation ready early, consisting of young men and boys. There was Brig. Gen. Kelly, Anson, and Hambel, who assisted in getting things arranged; Chaplain Babcock was bustling about with his white cravat, and making wonderful calculations as to the number of the wounded to be taken care of through the day. Judge Smith paced the upper chamber of the parson's house, fearful of the result as to taking the citadel by storm, after counseling soft words; while Ferguson, of Timber Creek, told stories of Indian wars among the Pottawatomies. Women had prepared breakfast with trembling hands, and partaken of it with tearful eyes and agonizing thoughts, fearing that ere set of sun, their loved ones might return mangled corpses or maimed for life. The excitement had spread all over the county, one orderly, Mr. C. Davis, having rode a great share of the night to rouse the Marshalltown army to immediate action. It is supposed there were eight or nine hundred men on the ground, either as combatants or spectators of the bloody fray.

The Marietta army was commanded by L. L. Weatherly, ex-sheriff, one of the best natured men in the world, and to see him now-a-days, one would not suspect him of belligerent propensities enough to kill a chicken. And so with the whole army, peaceable farmers and mechanics, all, but believing they were upholding the rights of the majority in the Marshalltown *posse;* while the Marietta soldiers fancied they were defending their Court House from thieves and robbers.

The Bowen Guards had sent by S. Curkhuff, to Fort Dodge and obtained arms, and being drilled, with Elliot Shurtz as captain, George Hampton as first lieutenant, and Wells Rice as second lieutenant, the whole company with their escort, cavalry and outriders, might be seen on the move about eight o'clock passing out of Main street, every door and window filled with sobbing women and children; there being no commissary or baggage for officers, and no artillery, the military pageant soon disappeared *beyant* the Western hills.

About ten o'clock, Mr. Gibson, another orderly, some

say as a Marietta detective, returned upon a handsome charger riding at a furious rate, when a score of voices yelled out, "Has any one been killed?" He shook his head mysteriously, and reported something to head-quarters, commanded by Major-Generals Woodbury and Henderson. After talking around town awhile, he mounted his horse and rode rapidly down the Marietta road to the scene of the engagement.

We will now follow the Bowen Guards. They had no martial music; some whistled to keep their courage up, others sang Yankee Doodle and told hunting yarns, while a few, like Pat, kept up a "divil of a thinkin'."

In the meantime, Mr. Greener who had spent a little time at the Marshall House, found out there was a raid in progress, and sometime in the night mounted his pony and went on to Marietta to give the intelligence. Orderlies were sent in every direction, and every man capable of bearing arms in Liberty and Minerva townships was on hand sometime in the forenoon. A keg of powder was bought at some of the little stores up the Iowa river, by the contribution of many citizens of Marietta, and placed under the safe of the Court House, with a train and slow match ready to blow the raiders into atoms. Patterson, of Patterson's grove in Minerva, was high in com-mand, having been in the Mexican war, but ex-sheriff Weatherly was chief, and he gave orders that strict discipline should be kept through the attack. After locking the Court House, many stood on the steps awaiting the onset; many of the windows were filled with armed men, and even on the roofs of some of the houses might be seen belligerents ready for the fight.

The army of invasion had been preceded by a force of cavalry skirmishers that made their appearance about four o'clock in the morning, under the lead of Mr. William Bremner, we believe. Mrs. Boardman had a

gun on her shoulder, and one of the company, " Kim "
Cleaver, getting defiant, she intimated that if he said
any more she would shoot him.

Other Marietta ladies were equally warlike, and the
excitement deepened in intensity.   J. Crookham,
the bachelor lawyer, made his will before the justice,
and then stood trembling near the Shively House,
awaiting the attack.   Mr. Dishon and Quincy Black
were on hand, with pistols at home, to defend their
firesides, for the threat had gone forth if the records
were not given up, " the town would be reduced to
ashes."   Mr. Woodbury and Mr. Henderson had no
idea of this, nor Mr Rice, Anson or Doctor Glick—
their intention was to intimidate.   But Scott and his
gang of irresponsible men, taking advantage of this,
were no doubt intending mischief.   And many too,
allowed their feelings to get the better of their judgment, so that the result was, a desperate, murderous-
looking set of men entered Marietta, determined on
having the records, or burn, murder and destroy.

Many of the young boys of the village had rifles,
some had hatchets and axes, and we give the comic
side also; a man by the name of Daly, was seen
armed with a sausage-stuffer squirting muddy water
at the invaders.

Harris came in first, with a few men as body guard,
and presented his order very courteously to Mr.
Weatherly, who refused, of course, to give up his
trust.   Wagon after wagon followed, filled with armed
men, who dismounting walked around the streets
looking fight, if nothing more.   The Bowen Guards
had halted near town till about twelve o'clock, and
being hungry became anxious to fight or go home.
Harris was to come back and tell them when to advance, but he was cowardly and vascillating, so that
no order ever came to Captain Shurtz to move forward.
At last the Captain thought best to go on and see what
was doing in the beleaguered city; and the historic

page of war was made brighter by the advance of the
Bowen Guards to the Public Square. They were
forty as brave men as ever carried muskets, in appear
ance.

The women and children flouted and jeered at
the poor Guards from the windows, some threw decayed eggs and vegetables, fragments of brick and
stone ; and the contents of a huge wash-bowl fell upon
the head of a devoted citizen of Albion, Hon. T.
Brown, who was sandwiched among the soldiers.

THE ONSET.

Harris then commenced bustling about, and drawing
up a number of wagons for breastworks, told Captain
Shurtz to bring his men into line behind them.
Among them were Messrs. Taft, Hepburn, Kelly, and
other prominent citizens of Marshalltown. Slowly
the Guards advanced, with officers Shurtz and Rice
in front. The Marietta men cocked their rifles, and
when within about sixteen feet of each other, there
was not a sound to be heard but a click of guns.
Hepburn looked at the right, at the left, and seeing the
Guards flanked on every side, knowing that not ten
feet off stood an enemy with his hand on the trigger,
who had an old grudge to settle, he became suddenly
aware of the fearful consequences, and calling out to
Weatherly, "For God's sake, don't shoot !" threw up
the sponge.

Mr. Sylvanus Rice, a moment before, had narrowly
escaped trepanning from a cane being thrown at his
head, and Mr. Aleck Crow was about to slip the
mortal coil of a Guard, when Sam. Hoffman advanced
a little from the line and drew a bead, saying, "I'll
make a *white* Crow of you, sir, if you are not
careful."

The crisis was ready to burst its rain of blood upon
these deluded men of Marshall county, when Boardman

advanced a step or two, and in a loud, clear voice, with his inevitable imperturbation, read the injunction from Judge Thompson, restraining all action of removing the records; and with a higher authority than sheriff or guard, dispersed the crowd with a *benedicite* unlooked for, and which was really welcome to some, no doubt. The Bowen Guards slipped rather precipitately from the *cul-de-sac* in front of the Court House; and some swearing and loud talking being heard in another direction, the swaying crowd thinned out in this place.

Scott with his gang, had tried to set a building on fire with bundles of hay, but fortunately did not succeed, and one of the Guards in watching this movement, and thinking he might assist, jumped over a yard fence and tore his drapery in a vexatious manner, the only *abattis* the Guards found.

Captain Shurtz now ordered his men to "fall in," and the militia were soon en route for Marshalltown—Harris not to be found. One valiant Marietta man now emerged from behind a pile of rails, another took his gun from the window, where he had been watching the fight, a half mile distant. One Guard came into the ranks, who had the stomach-ache fearfully, through the onset; another had to light his pipe—"be back in a minute," but his minutes lengthened into hours. But the most were real belligerents, for in the defense of the old flag, men from the "Swamp Kingdom" and "Anson's potato patch," gave their lives freely, and were buried together on Southern soil.

Had there been a chance shot, and it is a great wonder that among so many boys, none fired; had Harris in the first flurry, rushed his men into the Court House and commenced breaking locks, there is no telling what horrors might have been committed. There is no mistaking this, and Providence certainly must have watched over these half-crazed men.

Outsiders began to talk over the injunction and com-

pare notes, some swearing at the judge for spoiling
the fight; they finally followed the action of the Guards,
mounted their horses, filled the wagons, and drove
away.   At sunset, the contest was fairly over, no one
hurt, and Marietta was the county seat in spite of
guard or musket, wearing her diadem with undimin-
ished lustre ; she was every whit the queen of the
Iowa valley as before, without sending a single hero
to the shades of Valhalla.

THE RETREAT.

The Guards on their return, with cavalry, pickets
and signal corps in a Bull Run confusion, met, about
half way from Marshalltown, Judge Smith and Mr.
Woodbury, going to Marietta. The judge made a
speech, saying that he had done what he thought was
right, of his own free will, and was glad things were
as well off as they seemed.

We will not attempt to describe the thoughts of the
stalwart army as they approached the gates of Marshalltown, for here the tragedy ends in a farce.   The
Guards had marched up more than " one hill then
down again," had come home victorless and no scalps.
No county records, no ashes of Marietta buildings,
not a scratch or smell of gunpowder, but awful tired
and hungry.   " Where is your dead ? "   " Where was
you in the fight? "   These questions assailed the poor
Guards on every side.

Messengers had been coming into town through the
day, but still there would be false reports.   Among
them was one, that Wells Rice was killed, which of
course had made his family nearly frantic.   Although
he was foremost in the fray, he had returned safe and
sound.

Another messenger had reported the streets of Marietta were running with blood.   Naturally these
rumors had suspended all business; the ladies had

walked about from one house to another, trying to find some consolation in each other's courage, so that when the doughty army came home safe, the rebound from such a dismal strain was wonderful. Wives joked at the expense of their husbands, tea was got, and the meal ended under happier auspices than ever before in their households.

We have heard many ladies say, that going to the battle-fields of the South, was nothing so gloomy as that dreadful day at Marietta. They felt not the loss of the county seat, or of its prospective advantages at the evening's close, so the loved ones were at home safe.

Several quarrels came off collaterally, but as far as open fighting went, this was the last of the Marshall-town army.

It was thought the next morning in Marietta, that the raiders might return, and every precaution was used to guard the public property, but the plumes of the Marshalltown cavaliers were not seen, for it was believed that the injunction restrained all further action, and they were, after all, in favor of law and order.

But more was had of the pen than of the sword. The lawyers were busy, and at the April term of the District Court, following, the mandamus case came up again. There was a long trial on the injunction, and an attachment was issued against Judge Smith for contempt, but he appealed to the Supreme Court, which decided against him. At this District Court, Marietta had a band of men pledged to secrecy, and under promise to slay and destroy, if Marshalltown attempted to take the safe from the Court House, even if decided in her favor.

Previous to this, on the 13th of January, Judge Smith issued bonds to William Dishon on a contract to build a Court House, and to the tune of $26,000. Mr. Dishon went to New York and sold the bonds for

6

goods instead of building, and this mercantile trans-
action cost the county $8,000 to release the bonds.
The bond-holder offered by his agent, to Mr. C. B.
Rhodes, of Edenville, five hundred dollars if he would
use his influence to bring them to a par value through
action of the board of supervisors, though there had
been an injunction issued against the sale of them.
Judge Smith expected, at the time, that Mr. Dishon
would do what was right, we have no doubt, but he
was not careful enough in placing himself in the hands
of designing men.

We know that Marietta was fighting for her homes
and that the citizens of Marshalltown did many things
illegal to gain her ends, but there was a majority in
her favor.   The fault seemed to be, Marietta could not
nor would not *see it.*   This action was copied by Eldora.
A little town in Hardin county had a majority of three
over her, yet she would not, and never did, deliver up
the records, and for her pertinacity is down on the maps
to-day as the capital of that county.

The injunction case came up again at the June term
of the Supreme Court, and the December term also,
when the whole case was reviewed and argued, and
finally a decision was given in favor of Marshalltown,
which ended the whole controversy.

There is another reminiscence of this war which
we cull from the past.   Mr. James Hambel, in an
angry dispute with Mr. Gibson, told the latter, that
he had "an eye for looking up a rope."   This the
gentleman took as a threat, and forthwith procured a
warrant for the arrest of Mr. H.   Mr. Wimberly, the
deputy sheriff, being from Marietta was not personally
acquainted with the culprit, and on coming up to the
court house in Marshalltown, inquired of Hepburn
where he lived.   Shurtz standing by, knowing the
danger of Hambel, winked to Hepburn to keep Wimberly busy, then scudding around the building, hastened down to Hambel's to hide him.   At last Wim-

berly got impatient, and asked again where the rascal could be found. The polite lawyer pointed out a man chopping wood in the yard as if for dear life. "That's him," said he.

Wimberly rode up to the house, dismounted, and commenced reading the summons to a man in a green coat and plug hat. After hemming and hawing and looking at the papers, causing as much delay as possible, Shurtz suddenly looked towards the public square and said in a sly way, "I guess you are mistaken in the man, Mr. Hambel is in his grocery." The officer hastened in quest of his game at the grocery, but no Hambel could be found. "He is down to his barn, I *seen* him go," said an innocent youth. Mr. Wimberly rode up to the gate and seeing a man standing near the stable door, asked the person if he was Mr. James Hambel, of Marshalltown." "I am not," answered the wicked James, "but he is in the stable." The officer dismounted and went into the barn, but the culprit was invisible, of course. Coming into the daylight again, believing he was sold, he looked in the direction of Sam. Scott's house, where he saw a man with grey clothes, on a horse, the same that the person wore when he drove up the second time, denying his identity. Wimberly put spurs to his horse to overtake him, and then commenced as laughable a race as ever was seen.

The man with grey clothes was not to be caught —down one street, up another, neck and heels, until quite a little time elapsed and then the deputy finally caught the John Gilpin. "A'nt you Mr. Hambel?" the pertinacious officer asked. "Nary time; what are you eternally dogging me for?" answered Shurtz, and his great black eyes looked unutterable ugly things at him. Wimberly thought he had better start for Marietta at once, and he was not seen again in Marshalltown until the cars came in for the first time, when he took observations, never having seen a railroad or car before.

J. L. Williams was to have been arrested at the time of Judge Smith's incarceration, but he dodged the officer very successfully, hiding bohind the pantry door, and under the bed, till he wore out the patience of his pursuer, and was left to enjoy the sweets of home.

But the greatest martyr in the conflict, was Rev. Mr. Babcock, who made himself quite meddlesome on some occasions. He tried to coax Mrs. Judge Smith to come down to Marshalltown to live, but the Marietta ladies blocked his game, by showering decayed eggs upon his clothes and saddle. No doubt he wished for a Smithfield fire to heat water for cleansing purposes, as he retired from the angelic braves. Doctor Statler also received some mal-treatment a day or two after the battle.

Upon summing up the case, an impartial witness would rejoice at the end of the conflict, for beside the bitter hatred and the blight attending such a controversy, there was an enormous expense in the courts connected with the exciting drama. As early as 1853, Messrs. W. Rice and Anson, paid Atwater, of Marietta, a thousand dollars to identify himself with Marshalltown, and urge its claim in the District Court. His argument is said to be one of the most masterly documents of the kind ever presented to a legal tribunal—all bosh and sophistry, to be sure, from beginning to end, but it gave the contest wordy show for the rival of Marietta, which after seven long years of waiting was crowned with success. Atwater, we opine, got tired of battling, or else he was afraid the antagonists would eat each other up before they were done with it, for he disappears early from the theater of action and is not heard of after 1854, in the history of the county.

William Penn Clark, the counsel for Messrs. Rice, Anson and Woodbury, was paid five hundred dollars at one time; not being satisfied with this little sugar plum, has sued for five hundred more, and the suit is still hanging fire in the Supreme Court. Judge Cole, now of the Supreme bench, received at one time, two hundred dollars from Marietta; Crocker, the same amount; but we have mentioned a very small share of the expense. Messrs. Henderson and Boardman gave their services gratuitously; it was a sort of legal training for them *et gladiatour*, and served to make them the athletes they are in the profession.

After the decision of the Supreme Court, declaring that Marshalltown was the rightful capital, Judge Smith, accompanied by L. Williams, on the last day of December, 1859, willed that the disagreeable task must be done, of

REMOVING THE COUNTY RECORDS.

Hitching up six yoke of oxen, the long contested property was taken from its corner in the little Court House at Marietta, placed aboard a sled, and under cover of the evening's darkness, across the silent prairie, with the mercury ten degrees below zero, they finally came to Main street and with but little ceremony gave up their trust to the proper officers.

The New Year dawned upon a glad village when the joyful news was proclaimed to the citizens of Marshalltown that the crown had changed hands, to last forever. Forthwith messengers were sent in every direction with invitations to everybody in Marietta and elsewhere to attend a

NEW YEAR'S RECEPTION

In the newly baptized city. Such havoc as was made among the little pigs and great turkeys! the tables groaned with eatables; and after everybody ate and drank all they could, there were still baskets full of fragments to be taken up. Nothing was done by halves, many of the citizens of Marietta came down, and were met with cordial greetings, the hatchet was buried, and peace was made between the two cities. But an old Dutchman going home that night, was heard to say, " I'se sho glad vat sall I do ? I musht vip sumpotty ! I vip mein frow if ze peeg has pen fed, if not, I vip her, ennyhow ; I musht vip sumpotty for thar ees no Mayette to vip eny more ! "

Long before supper, cold and hot punch had been freely partaken of by *some* of the influential gentle-men, then whisky with water, whisky without water, sandwiched with good brandy, then water, wkisky and brandy again, till I am convinced from all ac-counts, that many faces wore the expression they did on the day when the blessed news came of the taking of Richmond. It was a perfect ovation to the people of Marietta. There was a large pyramid cake, with the words, " Let the hatchet be buried." Mr. Mercer said, "We'll not cut this cake, but leave the motto intact;" and all through the evening every toast and sentiment expressed, was of a fraternal character. It was reported Dr. —— eat pumpkin pie for an hour, it tasted so like his mother's "good *mince* pie." But

THE DEATH BLOW

Had been given to Marietta. Soon after, her wealthiest and most enterprising citizens sold out at a ruinous sacrifice, and went to Marshalltown to live, where they were heartily welcomed. The stores and shops soon followed, the brass band dispersed, the literary society was obscured, away sped the houses one after another down to the new city, which had become a vampire to suck its blood—the work of demolition went on, until now, Marietta, six miles from a railroad, dismantled and ruined, is left with scarcely a trace of her departed glory.

Most of the county officers were re-elected after the

removal from Marietta, and have held the trust ever since, and nearly all who came to Marshalltown, are among the most esteemed and wealthiest of her citizens.

HON. D. L. ARNOLD,

Late revenue assessor of the sixth congressional district, is one of these, and made an excellent officer for the Government. Probably he would have the portfolio yet, had not Andy "swung the circle," and sent the voluminous papers to the care of another worthy officer, his successor, Gen. T. H. Benton. Mr. Arnold is wealthy, yet kind to the needy, and has an unspotted reputation as a Christian gentleman.

T. ABELL, ESQ.,

The pleasant banker, who still buys and sells exchange as he did in Marietta, and spent, with others, a large amount of money to make that village the permanent metropolis, is one of Marshalltown's most prosperous and energetic men. Mr. Abell has been a great helper in the Presbyterian church, and was forward to give of his means to the Orphan's Fair.

Mr. Joseph Holmes, Doctor Waters, and Doctor Whealen, all came in due time to Marshalltown, also Mr. Thomas Mercer has a beautiful home there. He is a botanist of great scientific attainments and has unrivalled taste in flowers.

The old court house bought by Mr. Turner, left Marietta and settled itself on the south side of Main street, and holds up harness and saddles instead of papers and maps, and tells no tales of powder trains and the secret plottings of its former days. Mr. Crow's hotel where the Times office is located, feeds the brain of Marietta as it did the inner man. Mr. John Turner, whose untiring energy, with his partner, Mr. C. C. Stone, has built one of the heaviest hardware stores in the State, was a Marietta man, and did everything within mortal reach to make it a city. His worthy lady, a sister of the charming Mrs. Abell and the winsome "Minta," has done much in embellishments at our festivals and county fairs, and especially at the Orphan's Home Fair. We shall always thank the few who wrought so faithfully in the floral department for that isle of beauty in the ocean of sand and dust elsewhere. Mr. J. L. Williams and H. D., his brother, familiarly called "Jake," are seen at the county clerk's desk, as chatty and genial as they were ten years ago at Marietta. In fact, these we have mentioned, and many others, are among the very best citizens of Marshalltown. All bitter feeling has died away, and the past with its horrors and threatenings, only serves to excite a smile, for all are friends and united in every good work. We have only to mention that Boardman hobnobbed with Henderson in a week after coming here, went into a law partnership with him, and now sits around the green baize with T. Brown, Esq., who did as much to kill Marietta as any other man.

Marietta will again become a business point should the railroad be built now projected between Marshalltown and Eldora. The village has yet about two hundred inhabitants, a store, several shops, and an excellent school under the management of Mrs. Quincy Black, a lady of thorough scholarship and graceful manner. Her exhibitions always call out a crowded house. There is an M. E. Church under the pastoral care of Rev. Mr. Hayman; and no town in the county is surrounded by farms under such a high state of culture. The Catholic Church which was finished in 1861, was usually filled by an earnest audience from French Grove, and a large settlement on the Minerva, but it was made of poor material, and blew down about three years since, to the great annoyance of the communicants and Father Emmons, of Iowa City, who officiated at the altar. The architect was Mr. S. Marshall, now of the St. James.

This township is rapidly filling up with new settlers, has excellent public schools, and is every way a desirable point for farmers.

IOWA TOWNSHIP.

Iowa township is situated in the second tier from the Hardin line, contains some very good timber, while coal crops out along the banks of the Iowa river, and it also well watered by that stream and its tributaries. There are splendid farms in this township, where locust and cottonwood groves have been cultivated, making a good protection for stock and fruit, besides giving rare beauty to the landscape. Iowa is quite thickly settled and for a long time polled more votes than any other in the county.. Among the earliest settlers, who came in the year 1849, was Messrs. Philip Ballard, William, his brother, and Jacob Hauser.

Mr. P. Ballard relates his experience in getting to the prairie home in this wise: It was early in the spring, and when coming to the Iowa river it was found necessary to cross on a piece of ice by laying boards from shore to the ice, the horses were induced to cross over, then the wagon was drawn over by hand (after the goods had been removed), then over went the furniture, and finally, the wife and little ones. It was a marvel to every one in the vicinity how they crossed and without danger. The bears troubled his pigs and carried off a few of them, and in revenge he stole bruin's honey from the bee-trees.

If we had only space to tell of the frontier experiences which the families "over the river" had through the Indian war, the cold winters in their miserable little cabins, their thankfulness when they could buy a pound of coffee, it might make some of us who grumble, more contented.

Mr. Hauser was county clerk in its first organization.

Mr. Seymour was one of the earliest pioneers, but is now living in Kansas. But we will call the reader's attention to the most important place in the township, which is

ALBION.

It was laid out and surveyed in August, 1852, by George W. Voris and Thomas S. Brown, and given the name of Lafayette, which it continued to bear until 1858, when it was changed to Albion, there being another town named Lafayette on the Des Moines river. Albion is situated on the east side of the Iowa river, and has a splendid location, one of the finest in the State. Among the earliest settlers was Mr. Perrigo, now of Marshalltown, who had the first store here and helped build up Albion; Mr. Jotham Keyes, who did a large business on air foundations and then vanished from the board of trade. Attorney T. Brown, now law partner with Boardman, who is well known as one of the best criminal lawyers in the State; also, Professor Wilson, a talented editor and elocutionist. Mr. E. H. CHAPIN, whose witty, trenchant pen cuts evil and self-conceit right and left; Mr. Abram Stanley, a very successful business man, and Mr. Tripp, also a pioneer merchant, came about 1854, and all have been identified with the growth of the town.

About the year 1857, in the strife among the infant towns for notoriety and to become the county seat, Albion did not wish to be made a cat's paw by Messrs. Rice, Anson and Woodbury without a bonus, so having a literary taste, her efforts were put forth to obtain a seminary of learning. Upon a hint in the Iowa Central, whereof Mr. Chapin was editor, subscriptions were at once asked of the rival towns claiming to be the county seat; intimating that the one which gave the highest amount, would get the most votes from Iowa township in the coming election. Both went to work, and on presenting the subscription to the board of trustees of the Marshall County High School in Albion, it was found that Marietta had given three thousand dollars; and Marshalltown, not to be outdone, raised hers to one thousand more.

This commenced the present College building, but the county voted the sales of all swamp lands for the finishing of the enterprise, releasing all these stockholders from their engagements, excepting those from Albion. As many prominent men had given notes as well as money, it was quite a relief. Under some defect in the school law, it was found that they could get no help from the State, so that when the officers of an organization calling themselves the Iowa Lutheran College, offered to buy the high school building, it was sold to them, they representing that they had an endowment fund of sixteen thousand dollars. This was considered a fine stroke of diplomacy for Albion. Rev. E. Geiger was chosen president of the faculty, with several professors, etc. For some reason the endowment fund never reached the sum named above, and it has been struggling along to the best of its ability ever since. It has met a scathing ordeal of sectarian prejudice, also internal dissensions in the faculty; the citizens have often given it a *side wipe*, and it has had quite enough to wither the life from any corporate body of learning. It has, however, been very liberal to the soldiers, and had some faithful, self-denying teachers, but it needs an endowment fund of a hundred thousand dollars, and enough more in its purse to add a couple of wings to the old dilapidated structure, and refurnish it from turret to foundation with new furniture, apparatus, etc. We wish this institution of learning great prosperity, and hope that money will be raised for the above purpose.

A BREWING TEMPEST.

After washing the feet of Albion, after kissing the faces of their dirty children, after exhausting stores of snuff and tobacco for her old women, and giving them all the swamp lands and other material aid, Albion, in February, 1860, (after a submission of two months to Marshalltown as the rightful sovereign,) circulated a petition through the county, praying that the county seat should be removed to that place. Fearing that there might be a successful hearing before the county judge, and there would be the expense and trouble of another canvas, a remonstrance was likewise circulated, and learning through a faithful detective, that there was about as many names on the petition as upon the remonstrance, one night a committee, self-appointed in Marshalltown, drew up about four hundred fictitious names that could be used in case of an emergency. Some of the names were those of persons in their graves, some were in the Eastern States, and occasionally the surname was transposed with the baptismal cognomen, until the "hodge-podge" was well calculated to deceive a Philadelphia lawyer, but only sixty were used. The case came up before Judge Battin and it was on trial nearly a week. As soon as it was found that there might be a possibility of a decision in favor of Albion, (Judge Battin being a citizen of that village) it was thought best by the watchful guardians of Marshalltown to arm themselves with an injunction from the district court against removing the records. So in the darkness of the night, Esquire Gregg and Doctor Statler started for Iowa City to obtain a hearing of Judge Thompson, as he was going there to attend court. When within a few miles of the city they overtook him, and he, fortunately granted the injunction.

They returned quite elated with their success, but the document never was used, for Judge Battin thinking it was time the county seat insurrections should be crushed, decided against Albion, and threw the costs of the suit upon the plaintiffs, T. J. Wilson, Esq., Daniel Wheeler, Mr. Tiipp and a Mr. Sweet. This was the last eruption of the county seat fever, which promised to be chronic for some time to come, as it was alleged that Marietta was at the bottom of the conspiracy.

As a specimen of the sharpness of some of the Marshalltown men, we mention the fact, that while Mr. William Howard, of Liberty, was producing the petition at the trial, and giving testimony as to the genuineness of some of the names attached to it, a sly rascal cut off about forty names from the paper with his pocket knife, in the twinkling of an eye, passed it to another of the same Beelzebub persuasion, and with the aid of a couple of wafers, persons were made to do duty on the other side of the house. Mr. Howard and the court, were so occupied that they never noticed the deception, and probably it is not known to many of the county to day.

At this trial, the downcast looks of the plaintiffs was considered a good offset for the *unpleasantness* that Albion had caused Doctor Glick and Mr. Woodbury at their trial, for holding Judge Smith's nose to the grindstone.

PRIMITIVE LIVING.

Mrs. Perrigo mentions renting the first frame house built in Albion. Then they made preparations for a home, Mr. P. hiring a hand from Cedar Rapids to assist him in the project. The man got sick, so Mr. Perrigo built the house alone, raising the balloon frame by himself, mostly. Mrs. Perrigo remembers of moving into it when the roof was shingled only at one corner, and she could lie in bed and see the stars as they marched in solemn procession through the night. The shingle horse where they manufactured the shingles, stood next to the table, and pictures, tin skimmers, clothing and skillets were close neighbors on the unplastered walls.

Mrs. Perrigo once dressed in calico for an afternoon visit, wearing also a gingham sun-bonnet and cotton gloves. This costume was considered such an index to her pride, that it was made the subject of remark, especially the gloves, but Mrs. Arny, the hostess was glad to receive her, and she spent a pleasant afternoon with others of the company who would laugh at cotton gloves now-a-days, as well as Mrs. Perrigo, who is unrivaled in her taste for dress.

Mr. J. P. Allington came later, was an excellent mechanic, and at an early day, made wagons for the Iowa farmers. Mr. B. T. Phillips, a prominent man in this section, came in 1856, and has filled some of the first offices of the township with trust and ability. He is now an extensive stock and grain dealer. Mr. William Thrall, a good citizen, has been here some years.

Mr. Lucas built the first hotel in Albion, then sold to Mr. Hobart, and the location was long known as the Hobart House. Mr. Howell, of Ohio, bought it two years since, and in western parlance, he knows " how to keep hotel," or rather his wife does, for is not the landlady the central sun of the whole system in a *tarvern?*

One of the early settlers was Mr. Beeson, whose son, Lieutenant Beeson, served with so much distinction in the Union army; also Mr. Hunmalean, who set out a beautiful grove of cottonwoods and had fruit and stock in great plenty. He was a man of energy; although wasted by long sickness he still would work. Some one asked him not long before his death, why he kept planting ornamental trees. He gave a beautiful reply, "Some weary body will love to sit under their pleasant shadows and think of me when I am gone." He placed in the solid earth a more splendid monument than the costliest marble column, which will outlive his worthy act for generations to come.

The first newspaper published in Albion was edited by Prof. T. WILSON, now of Marshalltown, and called the Iowa Central Journal. This enterprise was commenced in the month of November, 1855. It was the only newspaper published in a radius of one hundred miles; and on looking over its files we find fine ability as a writer, and it certainly reflected great credit upon the Professor to place such a shining light in the darkness of the western border.

He afterward sold out to E. H. Chapin, Esq., who associated with him, R. H. Barnhart, a good local and a successful publisher, who has been in partnership with his brothers, publishing a line of democratic journals through the State. Mr. Barnhart at this time was a man of small means, his lady assisting him in setting type; and in the space of ten years has become wealthy. Iowa is the home for poor men. Afterward, Mr. Chapin sold to Doctor Taylor, a clear, pleasant writer, author of a former history of the county, and one of the earliest physicians in its limits. The office was moved to Marshalltown after the removal of the county seat, and was known as the Marshall County Times.

On the 4th of July, 1855, everybody and his wife were invited to a celebration of the natal day of the Republic, at the town of Lafayette. The multitude assembled on the Public Square; Mr. Sawyer now living in Marshalltown was chief marshal of the day, Doctor Hixon gave the oration and read the Declaration of Independence. William Ballard and a few others did the singing, and it was a good time. Doctor Whealan was to have taken the forum, but in passing a new building, a wicked shingle in its downfall struck him on the head, so that he failed to perform his *role*, and gain immortality as a speaker— he never attempted the like again, believing that Fate had other employment for the exercise of his talents. On another occasion, in 1857, Judge C. C. Cole gave the oration, and a Mr. Lloyd read the declaration, but spoiled all by attempting to explain the meaning of that sublime yet perfectly simple document in a long harangue. Mr. Ballard (who, by the way, has a beautiful voice), also gave " Hail Columbia " at this celebration. Some years after, when a company of soldiers were leaving for the field, he sang the " Old Liberty Tree," with fine effect upon the crowd.

In the year 1859 there was a Congregational Church formed in conjunction with Marietta, Rev. E. Boardman, pastor, who officiated alternately in that capacity once in two weeks. There was a membership of fourteen. Mr. P. Chapin, a man full of Christian graces, now living in Marshall, was chosen deacon, and another good man, Mr. M. Hastings, was their secretary. The Lutherans coming in 1861 in such numbers, it was thought best to disband, and, with a few scattering Presbyterians, sacrifice on the same altar with them. Mr. George Keyes, one of the members of this little church, was noted afterward for his bravery in the army. A Mr. Larrison was killed in building a bridge in this township, and his death was very much regretted at the time. Mr. David Randolph, a prominent gentleman, came in 1856 to Albion, with his son-in-law, Mr. Cowgell, the superintendent of the M. E. Sunday School in their pretty brick chapel. Mr. Swearingen, quite a wealthy gentleman, and one of the trustees of the college, has been here some years. Judge Hobbs is now a resident of this township, and Doctor Richey, a good physician ; also Mr. Hinman, who has a splendid stock farm. He has been associated in business sometime with David Wells, one of the most noted stock dealers in the State. Lieutenant Arny of this township died a few months since, and was much beloved for his patriotic and noble bearing in the army and at home.

HON. H. E. J. BOARDMAN, RESIDENCE

North of Albion and further up the drowsy river, is a postoffice hamlet called Norris. It is of great convenience to the farmers in that thickly settled community. Mr. S. Meyer, one of the Fort men, lives in this section; he came from Tennessee originally, and settled here in 1853. He gave a brave boy's life for the old flag at Atlanta, who no doubt learned the lessons of freedom amid the mountain tops of the Cumberlands.

Judge Battin came to Albion sometime in 1856, and is favorably known in the county as an impartial, faithful officer, as well as an honest merchant. He has been thoroughly identified with the enterprises of the Iowa valley to develop its resources and make this section a desirable home for our people.

Mr. Cripps has decidedly one of the finest apiaries in the State. He sells hundred of pounds of honey yearly, that delicious epicurean dish, which is within reach of every dweller upon the prairie; also, grapes rivalling those of Eshcol, Guinea pigs and hens, and other useful animals He certainly will reap a pecuniary harvest for his labors and enterprise in this direction.

Albion has two stores, a grocery, hotel, and all the shops necessary for the wants of its citizens. It contains about four hundred inhabitants, and the advantages of the Lutheran College make it an attractive point to settlers. They have several churches in organization, and service is generally held in the college building. Rev. Dr. Sternberg lectures to crowded houses upon religious topics, which is of great benefit and enjoyment to the citizens. We bespeak for this beautiful little town and for its infant college an abundant prosperity.

MARSHALL

Township is a little east of the geographical center of the county, and is rolling prairie dotted with splendid groves, with Asher's Creek, Linn and the Iowa ot,

7

water the surface, making it a natural garden supplying the market of Marshalltown.

The earliest settlers were two brothers, William Ralls and G. S. Ralls, also John Braddy and Mr. Crowder.

The first white child born in this township was Joseph Luther, a son of Mr. G. S. Ralls, and he is still living in Iowa township. William Ralls came from Wapello county in March, 1850, and lived in a cabin near Colonel Shurtz's present residence. Soon after their arrival their house was robbed and burned, leaving the family almost destitute. As many of the valuables was afterwards seen in a canoe, there was not much doubt as to the authors of the mischief. It was a cruel thing under the circumstances. They lived on a dirt floor in a cabin afterward, had a tough time through the Indian war; but in a few years made a good farm and now are wealthy. The first court and county election was held at their house, and there were just thirty votes in the ballot box.

" Jack " Braddy had a claim and cabin a little west of them. He cut poles about as large as a stove pipe and made his home, covered the roof with slough grass, and himself and family had a terrible contest with ague here. It often rained down in torrents on their shaking frames, and those who have had the ague can properly appreciate their situation.

Mr. Washington Asher, another pioneer on the northern edge of the township, had a claim near the creek that bears his name. It is a beautiful stream and is noted for its splendid ice in winter and purple grapes in autumn. After Mr. Asher's people came out of the fort, the *gude man* was away on business a part of the season. So afraid was Mrs. A. of the snakes, that on retiring she used to place the chairs in a row to walk upon in case she was obliged to light the candle in the night.

Mr. Thomas Brown, who went into the army and

died in some far off hospital, is often mentioned as one of the earliest settlers in this neighborhood. The family lived on cracked corn and wild meat for a long time. He rendezvoused with the others north of the river at the time of the Musquaquan war in 1850, at P. Ballard's house. He was a brave, good man in every particular.

In the spring of 1854, there was another Indian scare called the Sioux war. Quite a large number of warriors assembled in Hardin county, and were often insolent in their demands, and the report spread over the prairies, that they were determined on driving the whites from the Iowa valley. The Indians certainly had an inextinguishable affection for Marshall country. Many of the settlers became very much alarmed and huddled together for protection for a day or two, at Mr. Brown's. But the Sioux soon changed their minds, and withdrew to the northwestern part of the State, where their smouldering hate flamed out in the massacre at Spirit Lake.

A Mr. More came a good deal later, about 1855, in this section, and built a good saw mill, which was of much advantage to the people. He owned a large claim of valuable timbered land, but after a few years of contest with western life died, much regretted. Mr. Brown is known, however, as having endured a great deal of privation. He came in 1849.

It is wonderful what powers of endurance many of these old settlers had! They shame us of a later day with our feebleness, for their feet were often frozen taking care of stock and procuring fuel; they had fevers and agues, but still wrought on their farms, shaking like bean pods in a November breeze. But the ague has almost entirely disappeared, and we have a very healthy country at present, and with the agricultural machinery, farming is now almost like play.

Mr. Silas Chorn is mentioned as coming to Marshall in the spring of 1852, and settling on a farm west

of the city, near Mr. Johnson Allen's. He is
employed at present at Mr. Turner's hardware
store; a man of strict probity in business relations.
Mr. Henry Hartwell came in 1854 and lives in that
neighborhood. Mr. H. is an exceedingly charitable
man. He was known for many years as making the
first brick in this section. He is a staunch Universalist,
and on all occasions maintains what he believes is truth,
without fear or restraint.

About here—sometimes called the half-way house
to Marietta, on what is now the edge of the corporation of Marshalltown—lived Mr. Allen. Also Mr. N.
Gillespie, well known as a strict temperance man, and
devoted Presbyterian. At one time the liquor sellers'
minions girdled a splendid orchard belonging to Mr.
G., worth two thousand dollars.

Another good family, members of the M. E. Church,
and loyal to the government, who came in 1854, and
identified with all good works, is old Father Canfield's
While living on his farm, the war broke out and three
of his sons went into the service, all making their
mark as brave, good soldiers.

HENRY ANSON, ESQ.,

Made the first settlement upon the present site of
Marshalltown in the spring of 1851, entering the
claim at the land office at Des Moines the same year.
Previous to this, however, there was a squatter who
had a little cabin on the south side of the claim.
Taking fifty dollars from Mr. Anson, he left, and went
away before Mr. A. built his cabin where Wiley's carriage shop now stands. His claim, however, was
bounded by the north side of Main street; and between
that line and the river, the land was owned by Mr.
William Ralls, who sold it to Mr. John Kelly, and
he, in turn, sold to Dr. John Childs for four hundred
and fifty dollars, property worth now nearly a half
million. Mr. Childs lived in a cabin on the north side

of the claim, but after the town was laid out he moved it upon Main street.

Was surveyed in the summer of 1853, long after Marietta, by Mr. Risden of Iowa City, under direction of Messrs. Anson and Childs, we believe. It was named after Marshall, Michigan, Mr. Anson having some pleasant memories of that place.

Mr. Anson was a son-in-law of Mr. Sylvanus Rice, of Trumbull county, Ohio, and he persuaded Mr. R., his sons Wells and Miles, also John A. Kelly, a brother-in-law, to make Marshall their home. This was in the spring of 1852. It is said of Mr. Anson, that after travelling over a considerable portion of Iowa, he came here, and in a fit of enthusiasm swung his hat over his head, " I 've found the prettiest place in the world," said he, " Here I 'll lay my bones ! " The families above-mentioned with Doctor Childs, were the founders of Marshall, the affix of *town* being added as there was another town in Henry county by the same name.

The first glass window in the township that let in the blessed sunlight, was framed in Anson's cabin. Many of the settlers thought it a useless piece of furniture, as they lived with open windows the year round. Mr. Anson was known as the red-headed Yankee, who had a well-sweep, and that *machine* was talked of as another useless thing, for a rope was cheaper, if not so handy. Some of his relatives coming a year or two after, (Mrs. Anson and " Mike " as he is familiarly called) heard of " Hank's " well-sweep for ten miles eastward. Hank also proved himself quite a dentist, extracting teeth with a pair of bullet moulds. He built the first saw-mill on Linn creek and about the first one in the county, but it was burned in June, 1856, after being of great advantage to settlers. Mr. Anson was also the first Justice, and at the township election held in the embryo city, the voters dropped their ballots into a box through the window of his cabin.

When Mr. A. occupied this cabin in the north of the town, he was also Land Agent as well as Justice, and besides all the business carried on, the cooking for three families went forward under the same roof— the two brothers, Platt and Charley Smith from Iowa City, and the Squires of Marshalltown. Anson's mother and sister came in a year or two afterward. While they were building their cabin they lived in a wagon-box, placing the bed under the running gear of the wagon, with a couple of boards for shelter. They used to laugh at their airy dormitory as they bundled up for the night.

Mr. Anson built the present McLean House and has been connected with almost every prominent enterprise of the city and county.

DR. JOHN CHILDS,

Formerly of Ohio, came here the next year after Mr. Anson, and buying the claim of Mr. John Kelly, lived there and dispensed hospitality to many of the new comers. What appetites emigrants used to have in those days! Coming in wagons and through the bracing, healthy air of Iowa, dyspeptics lost their bad symptoms and took another form of disease, called the " Iowa eatables," or consumption, that is, *consume* all on the table and speak of kissing the cook. Railroad traveling is not half as good for dyspeptics as the old-fashioned canvas-topped wagon.

The first meeting held in Marshalltown congregated in Mr. C's cabin, which was thirteen feet square. A Cumberland Presbyterian minister on his journey stopped with the family, and consented to preach, it being the Sabbath. Mr. Childs moved the furniture outside, but still many were obliged to stand out of doors ; about thirty attended the services, and without any flattery to the preacher, he had, indeed a *crowded* house. Some of the boys and large girls were barefoot, and a large sprinkling of pasteboard sun-bonnets were to be seen.

We shall speak further of Mr. Childs in the unfolding of the history of Marshalltown.

SYLVANUS RICE, ESQ.,

Mr. Anson's father-in-law, came here in 1852 and built a barn which he used as a house until he could do better. There were no mills then, or lumber, so that the primitive logs and puncheons were the building material, excepting that brought from Iowa City. Mr. Rice afterward built a frame store, then the "Rice Hotel," of brick, and the Marshall House, with other enterprises of the kind. Mr. Rice has one of those cheerful happy natures which makes a new-comer feel at home and welcome. When he was landlord, this was very apparent, and his homesick neighbors who came early and had privations, often looked to him for encouragement and cheer. His estimable lady was very much loved in this vicinity; she died in 1863. He has since been united to a Mrs. Lord, relict of the late Doctor Lord, of Hardin county, and is now living there. His son, Miles Rice, is now living here, after two years' residence in Idaho.

WELLS RICE, ESQ.,

One of the founders of Marshalltown, is a citizen who has been more closely identified with her interests than any other for the past fifteen years. We mean no injustice to any one. Mr. Rice has never left the work of upbuilding the city for the time mentioned, has left no stone unturned, whereupon to lay the foundations of Marshalltown broad and wide. He came here in 1852 and lived in a cabin near the north end of what is now Mr. N. Gillespie's farm. The door was made of rived shingles, no latch, leaky roof, and crevices so large in the puncheon floor, that the little ones crept shyly past, for fear of the snakes and other *varmints* who sometimes took refuge there. Mrs. Rice came home one day and found a large rattlesnake cosily taking a snooze upon the door step, but she soon obeyed Scripture in despatching the gentleman to his own place, by bruising his head with a garden spade. Soon after the family came here, a beautiful little boy was born to them, whom they named Marshall after the embryo city, but he died after three months of life, and was buried on the Jack Braddy farm.

Mrs. Rice relates a legend of the early times in this wise. A lady had occasion to visit a neighbor, and on her return she found that she had left the door ajar. The woods near at hand were filled with hogs of a peculiar breed called "prairie sharks" brought here by the Indians. This species of hogs is now nearly extinct; they have very long legs and noses, immense ears, and thin as a slab. Upon going into the house, the lady saw to her surprise, standing on its hind legs in front of the cupboard, with its musical jaws in motion, one of these prairie sharks eating bread and butter from the top shelf! It was a sight for a housekeeper, and the broomstick played an important part in the drama afterward.

Mr. Rice was the first Postmaster in the town, and this enterprise was established in the fall of 1854. The mail came upon an old two-horse wagon, at first weekly—then, after a few years have passed away, think of our facilities for receiving intelligence by car and telegraph!

Mr. Rice lived in Bureau county, Illinois, before coming here, and on the journey the family met with a funny mishap. In crossing the classic waters of an Iowa slough, the horses mired down and wagon too. It was the last one on the trail and consequently was in a fair way to get to China, unless there was a long pull, and a strong pull altogether. After a half day's labor, by lifting with fence rails, the vehicle was righted up, but in the operation, overboard went a barrel of sugar, pickles, jars of sweetmeats, and a splendid rocking chair, into the ruins. We will not write further at present of Mr. Rice, but introduce another family to the reader's notice, early known in the village, whose name the *pater familias* bears, as

JOHN A. KELLY, ESQ.,

Who came here in 1853 and lived on a farm now owned by Mr. Edward Thayer, we believe. He built a cabin and had the usual furniture of those days ; for the experience of others had shown that fine uphol-stery was a poor investment to bring in a wagon for hundreds of miles, as our " Northwestern " was not a *carryall* for a good many years after. Mr. Kelly has amassed a splendid fortune, and with others has done much to develop the resources of the country, giving material aid to schools, the railroad, churches, and many other institutions.

Mr. Kelly gives the particulars of an exciting elk hunt which came off in 1852 that excels our Wall Lake friends in superiority of game. All of the set-tlers principally were engaged in it, and in the course of the day they brought down three large elk, wolves, deer, and coons without number. As it was in the winter, and snow on the ground, the game tracks were clearly perceptible, and there was a great deal of fun and hilarity on this occasion.

Mrs. Kelly and Mrs. Rice both have held high office in very many of the charitable societies in the city, and are ladies of great personal merit.

In this year came other actors on the stage ; among them,

C. B. STRAIGHT,

From Ohio, and built a cabin near North Main street, had quilts for doors, and the carpenter used wooden

8

nails instead of Pittsburgh, about the domicil. Mr. Straight helped initiate the contest for the county seat, and was prominent in building the court house and other improvements. He says many laughed at him as he wrought on the masonry of the court house, being so cold at one time that he nearly froze his hands as he laid the wall of the town hall, as it was ostensibly named at the beginning.

Mrs. Straight is one of the largest-hearted women in the world—kind to the poor and distressed everywhere.

Mr. Straight built a frame house, now occupied as a kitchen by I. J. Sanford, and then erected the beautiful Gothic residence which he now lives in, on West Main street. They have a nicely arranged flower plat, showing fine taste in its cultivation. In company with this family came Mr. S. Dwight, and upon buying the log house owned by Henry Anson, gave a tea-party soon afterwards to the citizens of the vicinity.

The next spring while Mr. Dwight was drawing rock, his little son, a lad of twelve years, fell from the load, and the wagon passing over him caused instant death. This was the first fatal accident in the county, and caused great gloom in the infant settlement. Mr. D. has a daughter that shows poetic talent, which, if cultivated, may make a future worth striving for.

In the summer of 1854 came Father Hoffman, one of the best men that ever lived in the city—is mentioned as dwelling in a rail pen with a slough-grass roof, and when it rained, Mrs. H. used to walk about her mansion under an umbrella. For a parlor, they arranged the family carriage by unloosening the curtains; and here too, " Mike," our deputy collector, had a long run of typhoid fever. Four of the family had the fever also, in consequence of exposure in this hut. So many settlers coming in, it was impossible to get lumber; but buying a house afterward, Mr. H. could not induce the proprietor to leave until he could obtain another house for *his* family. This frame house is the one now occupied by Mr. Hoffman. Mr. Yeamans and Mrs. Gillespie, Mr. Dubois, and Mr. Oviatt, who afterward married a daughter of Father Hoffman, came this year. Mr. Mead, also; and we think the good and much lamented Mr. Webster.

DISTILLERY.

About this time, an old gentleman by the name of Haynes, built a rude distillery in the northwestern part of the town, constructing his receivers of dug-out troughs of wood. Trappers would take a bag of corn and a jug, empty the corn into a heap, and fill the jug from the trough without a graduating scale or measure. Glorious days for topers!

AMUSEMENTS.

The young and old danced on the puncheon floors, and sometimes played "pussy in the corner." Before they had any church or Sunday School, the Sabbaths seemed long and lonely, excepting to a few devout believers. One lady says that they left their "go to meetin's on the other side of the Mississippi." There certainly was a woful lack of church privileges or even prayer meetings.

When Mr. Anson finished his mill, the citizens considered it quite a treat to go down by the brook-side and listen to the tic-tac and clatter of the much-needed institution.

Mrs. Childs relates a pleasing incident of going to the Iowa river one day with her little girls on a fishing expedition. It was her first trial. They had asked for fish, should she give them a scorpion? No! So, taking line, hook and bait to the running water, and hushing her partners in the expedition to a proper degree of silence, she succeeded in taking a huge red-horse, quite corpulent enough for the family's supper. Such self-reliance would have made a successful quartermaster even in the desert of Sahara.

It was splendid days for housekeepers then—no two weeks of spring cleaning, no ruffles to make or yards of tatting to crotchet ; they did not skate or turn up their noses at a mechanic's wife ; they did up their housework in short time and in order, then read over old letters and the New York Tribune, while the day ended with a social chat among their neighbors. It would be exceedingly dull now-a-days thus to live.

Henry Anson and Mr. Wells Rice, restless and ambitious, were not satisfied with their place being a suburb of Marietta, and as far back as 1853 commenced war on the aforesaid, with no more remorse than if plucking an owl in the forest. Atwater, of Marietta, was a keen lawyer, and one day he was approached by these powers behind the throne, and forthwith became a most devoted follower of Marshalltown. Then came a long argument that the location of the county seat at Marietta was illegal, as there were only two commissioners instead of three, according to legislative action. There were three more talked of, and when they were appointed by Judge McRay, each received a splendid shot-gun, so it was reported. Marshalltown then claimed the county seat to all new comers, which was as stoutly denied on the other hand by Marietta. These stakes were set in 1853. Finally, a writ of mandamus came from the District Court compelling Marietta to remove the records. All being *bosh* on the part of Marshalltown, just to keep the thing in law until they could control public sentiment to carry the question.

Anson and Rice, afterwards assisted by Mr. Woodbury and others, carried on this contest through seven long years, and finally their pertinacity was crowned with success.

It was the theme of many an anxious conversation among the citizens of the little village—let them but once get this advantage, the certainty of Marshalltown becoming a city was beyond doubt. There was nothing done by halves, everybody was treated handsomely, and an agreeable impression was sought to be be made upon the stranger, so that he might be induced to turn around his four-wheeled emigrant-ship with its freight of pigs, chickens and tow-headed children into the Marshalltown harbor.

Wells Rice built the first respectable building in the city, being made of lime, sand and gravel mixed together and called grout. This was in the fall of 1852. Dr. John Childs, of the firm of Choate & Childs, built the first frame house in the following summer of 1853. They celebrated its grand appearance on the corner of Main and Center streets, by a house-warming—without chamber floors, but *with* a "glorious supper and dance," as an actor in the festivities reports.

The first two-story frame store, (now occupied as a meat market near Dr. Cummings) was built by C. B. Straight, in company with Mr. Sylvanus Rice, the gentlemanly, stirring citizen who did so much in an early day for our city. The first brick building was put up by Charley Davis, and is still standing on the corner opposite Mr. Straight's residence on Main street. Mr. Child's building has been *transplanted* within a few years to the lot westward of Levi Page's cottage house, to make room for Abbot & Knisely's brick block.

Mr. Rice's cement store did not last but a few years in our Iowa winds, for it soon cracked, and went into disintegration and ruin. The two-story house now occupied by Mr. Hoffman was one of the first dwelling houses.

BIRTH AND DEATHS.

The first white child born in Marshalltown, was Adrian Anson, son of Henry Anson, Esq., in 1851.

The first funeral in the village was that of a little daughter belonging to Mr. Silas Chorn, on the 10th of August, 1853. It was a gloomy hour to the family, for there was scarcely a word of ceremony—they parted the wild grass and the yellow autumn asters at the corner of Jack Braddy's farm, with no prayer or death-song, but laid the little one to sleep in a pine coffin till the prophesied bright morn of the future. On the 10th of September following, her sister, a sweet child of seven years, was placed beside her in the same primitive manner. There was not a professing Christian in the neighborhood. At this funeral, Mrs. John Smith, mother of Mrs. Ralls, remarked she could not rest easy thus buried, but in the following January, she was interred in the same way. Mr. Caleb Braddy also buried a child the next spring without a word of ceremony, no shroud, nothing but its little calico slip for its grave cerements, and they drove away to the spot where the others found a resting place at a quick pace, and the last rites were soon despatched by the family.

WEDDING.

The first wedding here was a double one, and a joyful day it proved to the young couples, for they went down to Timber Creek, had a good supper, and came back to town in a two-horse buggy in great state. Everybody was on the lookout to see them return. The happy duos were Miles Rice and Miss Anson; Mr. Horace Anson and Miss E. Smith. This was on the 17th of September, 1854. In the same fall, old Mr. Rice started up a couple of deer near Linn Creek, turning them westward they took a gallop down Main street, printing their cunning little hoofs on the future mart of business. Many *deers* promenade there yet, but are not quite so *shy*.

PRIMITIVE LIVING.

Mr. Edw. Willigrod came in 1854 and built his cabin upon the site of Doctor Statler's present home. There was not a nail in it, and the slabs which covered the roof blew off one night in a terrible storm, and the family were obliged to rouse up in the pitchy darkness and find out the extent of the programme arranged by the storm king. Down went the chimney and away flew the chairs which set outside of the house, it being too small to hold the furniture and beds. This storm also blew down a house belonging to Mr. Webster which was in process of erection.

Mr. David Parret's family lived in the back room of the store occupied by Mr. Parret. It was a kitchen, parlor, music room, and dormitory for a family of seven persons. As these pioneers now occupy splendid residences, they can well laugh over their former mishaps. Many others lived in the same manner.

SABBATH SCHOOLS.

A Sunday School was organized this summer, with Mr. Yeamans as superintendent and John Kelly as librarian. This little nursery of the church counted but seven members at first. Father Dunton and Mr. Hoffman were often seen there, and almost everybody in the little town labored more or less for it, regardless of sect. It held sessions for sometime, but finally went down, and the effects were turned over to the Methodist Episcopal Church.

SINGING SCHOOL.

The first singing class in the town, was taught by Mr. Childs, composed of young folks, although some were " keeping company " and generally "sparkin' "

Sunday nights, so that they were learning lessons of Cupid, as well as the "do, re." One chap got jealous, and threatened to horsewhip the teacher if he interfered with some arrangements he had made with his sweetheart.

After this school, in 1853, Mr. Childs sold out the most of his claim to Mr. Webster, who was an excellent man, very benevolent, gave city lots away to poor men, and died in 1863, much lamented.

Mr. Childs became discouraged and went to Iowa City. He was sadly missed in the little village, and often regrets his "change of base," as his claim is now the center of the world.

The singing school had no leader until Professor Heighton came a year or two afterward.

Music was often enjoyed as one of the fine arts at the social gathering, and in little expeditions to the forest for berries and wild apples, the voices of singing boys and girls rang out on the summer air. We record a laughable affair which we name the

BLACKBERRY HUNT.

There had been rumors of fruit across the river, so Mrs. Willigrod, Mrs. Bissell and a few others started out with a team, Mr. Pratt as driver. Mrs. Willigrod prudently put on a pair of her husband's boots for fear of snakes. On arriving at the canoe the whole party arranged themselves with Mrs. Willigrod in the stern. They amused each other by laughing and singing, also by plashing water on Mrs. W. She, to avenge herself, threw many handfuls from the river into their faces, but just as the boat struck the opposite bank, in reaching to give them a final baptism she fell backward into the river, *boots* and all. The party laughed, but like the frog in the fable it came very near being the death of her, for she rose the second time before the stupefied Mr. Pratt could rescue her from the peril-

ous situation. Coming out of the water like a drowned
kitten, she was glad to make her way home without
any blackberries. Mrs. Willigrod has such a vein of
genial humor, one enjoys an hour of her experiences
in border life.

We cannot chronologically arrange many things
illustrating the pioneer times, but in this connection
we mention a

TEA DRINKING

At Mr. Sylvanus Rice's hotel, when the chamber floors
were not laid, or the partitions up. All the ladies in
town were there, and Mrs. Rice had a quilt in the
frames. Mrs. Calvin Straight wore a very pretty black
and white gingham, and one of the neighbors hung
back and would not go, for Mrs. S. was dressed so finely,
that it "shamed her calico," she remarked. This was
before the age of hoops, waterfalls, seventy-five dollar
dresses, etc., which we see at the tea-parties of to-day.
Among the ladies present, was Mrs. Polly Gillespie
of the M. E. Church, who came in the spring of 1854.
There was also Mrs. Oviatt, who died not long after.
Mrs. Henry Anson, whom everybody loved and admired, also Mrs. Willigrod and Mrs. Bissell. It was
a happy day, but alas! hostess, and more than
half of her guests, have gone to the land of forget-
fulness.

Mrs. Rice was an excellent woman, and her exem-
plary life gave no opportunity for criticism; when
she died she had not an enemy in the world; and the
same may be said of her daughter, Mrs. Anson.

FOURTH OF JULY.

The first celebration of our nation's birth day held
in the county was on the public square in Marshalltown in 1853. Invitations were extended throughout
the Iowa valley, and as many as could availed them-

selves of the opportunity to recognize this anniversary of the Republic. There was a large bower built of green waving branches, the starry flag waving gaily over all; tables were spread with all the delicacies that could be obtained, and everybody wore a joyous look, for the guests were splendidly entertained; the citizens having a sharp eye on the county seat, as well as their patriotism, felt it their duty to welcome all with smiles and cheers. An old lady was present by the name of ——; on hearing Doctor Bissell, who was chief marshal, call for cheers, she shoved a young girl out of a chair very suddenly, with " Don't ye hear them call for *cheers?* Git up, aint ye no manners ! "

Mr. Atwater, the young lawyer of Marietta, delivered the oration, and the singing class of Mr. Childs gave the crowd, " Hail Columbia," in fine style. Mrs. Choate, then a little girl in the choir, was obliged to stand upon a box, so that her head should be level with the rest of the soprano singers.

Many of the visitors were loaded with *goodies* on their return home, filling red and yellow cotton handkerchiefs and tin buckets; some coming twenty miles.

The lady committees, which comprised the most of the women in town, saw the sunset, very much fatigued. Old Mrs. Rice trimmed the cake as happy as at a wedding; Mrs. Straight remembers filling a clothes basket full of good things for the table, and many others wrought hard and gave much for the same object.

CONCERT.

Pursuing the same subject of amusements, without reference to dates, we note the fact, that the first public concert given in Marshalltown was by a singing class trained by Professor Heighton. The choruses were sung by the whole class, the solos, duos and quartettes were rendered by the beautiful Miss

Cleavers, twin sisters; Mrs. Andrews and Miss E. Hopkins as the alto. Professor Heighton played the accompaniments upon a melodeon with his own musical grace of to-day, and the audience were delighted with the entertainment.

There were no librettos or opera glasses then in the audience. Harry Gerhart, our able county treasurer, played the violin and sang bass in fine style. It was a pleasant affair to all concerned. Professor Heighton has done much to elevate the standard of music here, having organized all the choirs in the city churches excepting the Disciples. Prof. Montgomery and lady, Mrs. McClure, and Miss Nettie Cole, gifted singers among us came much later. Miss S. Montgomery has assisted Prof. Hughes, a blind musician, through a series of successful concerts in Wisconsin and Northern Iowa.

But we turn a leaf backward on our record to 1852, and talk of our

PIONEER MERCHANTS.

We have mentioned that the first store was built and filled with goods by Wells Rice, Esq. Mr. Pratt, member of a firm from Iowa City, also sold goods here; he is principally remembered as having a huge shock of red hair, and being an easy sort of man. Mr. E. Willigrod, from Mansfield, Ohio, came in July, 1854, bringing a small stock into the little shop now occupied by a gunsmith, east of J. L. Williams' residence. At this time there were only seven respectable buildings; a weekly mail, often delayed, and no mode of transit except across the horrible sloughs. But with prophetic foresight, these merchants struggled on, believing in the future of Marshall county. Mr. Willigrod promised his wife when they drove into the little hamlet that she would see the cars in ten years. Sure enough, in nine years they whistled through a city. Mr. Pratt became discouraged, and left. A Mr. Young came in the fall and sold a few goods in the building once occupied by Mrs. Holt as a millinery shop. Mr. Enos Hoes, previous to this, built the first frame store, at Dr. Cummings' corner. All the lumber and nails of the building were brought from Rock Island. In partnership with him, was his brother, Job C. Hoes, of Chicago, and after trading awhile they sold out to C. B. Straight.

Selling on credit, it was a matter of some doubt whether merchandising would be a success in the long run. Mr. Webster, we will remark, was buying and selling real estate this same fall. Considerable emigration came into the county and town. Mr. Westcott, from Maine, one of the pioneers, bought three acres of Mr. Webster, also a little house of Charley Smith.

In the fall, the house now occupied by S. S. Miller, was built by Mr. Yeamans, and Mr. Utz's present home; the frame buildings now numbered eighteen, all told.

As the rivalry with Marietta was constantly kept up, and the stakes set here for a county seat by the bosh commissioners, the spires and turrets of another Chicago rose before these energetic and ambitious men. Mr. Andrews, Mr. Crowder and some others, who have gone away since this season we have noted, played quite an important part in the early growth of our city. We do not know the exact time, but Mr. John Kelly built the shoe store now occupied by G. W. Peet, and had quite an establishment for early times. Mr. Hoes, as we have intimated, got tired of selling goods, and sold to Mr. Straight, who, in company with old Mr. Rice, had built the two-story frame, a little west, and had a small town hall above, where dancing parties often met, singing classes held jubilees, and the Musquaquas had pow-wows.

In time this building changed hands into the possession of Mr. M. Anson, who filled up with liquors and groceries. Mr. Willigrod built a store between the corner and this, now owned by David Woods; he had also drugs and patent medicines, sold dry goods, too, and Dr. Glick coming soon after, we hear of the firm of

GLICK & WILLIGROD,

In 1856. They were very genial and pleasant in their business relations, and from small beginnings have amassed fine fortunes, and occupy a prominent position in society. Dr. Glick practiced medicine in the city in early times, but, it seems, did not like the profession and was appointed postmaster, holding the position for some years. He is also our school fund commissioner; and without doubt has the most artistically arranged drug store in the State. One could easily imbibe all sorts of vile nostrums amid so much beauty and taste. After Dr. Glick went into the drug store, Mr. Willigrod associated with him Mr. Louis Willigrod, also from Mansfield, Ohio, and was found in the first brick building on the north side of the public square, built by him at considerable cost.

In the year 1854, Mr. Wells Rice took the dry goods store of Mr. Hoes and sold goods on Dr. Cummings' corner, then the center of the town. Calico was a "bit per yard." "Bit a yard," inquired an Eastern lady at this time, "What kind of an animal is a bit, Mr. Rice?" The Hawkeye merchant, with great *bon hommie*, explained that a "bit," in commercial parlance, was a shilling. But Mr. Rice has grown wealthy, selling calicoes at "a bit a yard."

But we will cross the street from the Cummings' block, and in the little building, west of Bishop's blacksmith shop, had we looked into the large windows just eleven years ago, we might have seen Mr. Joseph Smith, now a merchant of Eldora, selling boots and shoes of his own manufacture, and a few from Iowa City of Eastern make.

DAVID E. PARRET,

Now one of the directors of the National Bank, and a successful merchant, sold goods in a little building since used as a stable. It was westward from Mr. Smith's shoe store, and then on the fashionable side of the street.

"West End" was once the center of trade, but after Mr. Woodbury built his brick block and the Court House was finished, the star of empire in Marshalltown business rose where all other stars do, in the east, though there may be a retrocession when Mr. Rice finishes his new brick block. We will mention, *en passant*, that Mr. Ambruster had a shoe store also at the West End.

In the old stone shop where Mr. Dean works in paints and oils, delved as the first blacksmith, a Mr. Hill, who has gone to the "other shore."

Dr. Bissell was the first practicing physician, having come to Marshalltown in 1853. He was shot some years ago by a Mr. Coble, through jealousy. There were some grounds for the homicide, and Coble served a few years in the State prison and then went into the army.

Esq. Gregg is claimed as the senior lawyer, and barring some errors in politics is an honor to the bar, and an excellent citizen. Dr. Taylor came about the same time, and the two boarded at the Marshall House as chums and fellow bachelors.

After Mr. Rice built the Marshall House, which, by the way, has received several additions to the original structure, he rented to Mr. Morrison of Michigan, who kept the hotel sometime, then sold to Mr. L. Anson, and he sold again to Mr. H. D. Ranney in 1859. Mr. Ranney came to Iowa, however, in 1857, and built the store now occupied by Mr. East as furniture rooms. It was all prairie eastward for a mile, and the ladies when they shopped could study landscape views also.

Mr. Ranney's father came afterward with his family ; also, Mr. Leach, a brother-in-law, a very successful merchant. Mr. East, another brother-in-law, came later, in 1862 ; he has been of great help in the church and society. We cannot refrain from adding a word for his worthy lady who accomplished so much at the State Fair here.

J. M. Sherwood, Esq., came about the year 1857, also, and is well known as a pleasant, wealthy lawyer, giving generously to all public and private charities— his lady gracing the splendid Gothic residence on the east side of the public square.

And Dr. Bunce seeing the community needed another physician, came the next year after Dr. Glick. He had a large practice, often riding twenty-five miles over the prairies.

Mr. Gettings, from Castalia, Ohio, also added to the energy and activity of business in Marshalltown. And as we gossip of the pioneers further, we will notice Mr. James Hambel, who opened a grocery, and was in the stock and grain trade for a good many years. He came in the year 1857.

MR. S. LACY,

Long one of the most useful members of the Methodist Episcopal church, came to Iowa in 1856 and settled on a farm, now owned by Mr. Pontius. There was a cabin, but Mr. Lacy not liking to till the soil left the farm and came to Marshalltown in the summer, and was soon after, we believe, in company with Mr. Utz, in a grocery.

Mrs. Lacy the acknowledged leader of the *haut ton* taught the first select school in the village, and a very good " school marm " she made, too, the citizens valuing her services highly in that direction.

Mr. Chester Heald came earlier, in 1855 ; and it is almost superfluous to speak of many of these prominent and useful citizens, they are so well known for every virtue. Mr. William Johnson is another good man, one of the first blacksmiths in the city—has grown wealthy in working at the forge. Mr. Levi Page who buckled the first harness together for our markts, now at the head of an extensive establishment, came here in 1857. The next year, Dr. Statler, from Mansfield, Ohio, went into partnership with John Wasson, Esq., in a drug store—the first in town. They occupied the building now used by Duguid & Fuller.

About this time came John Fisher and opened a dry goods store soon after he became a citizen. Mr. Fisher had a good deal of public spirit in connection with churches and schools, although he was a little arbitrary in matters of opinion. He was very upright in his dealing with his fellow men and filled the office of Mayor at one time.

Mr. T. Hopkins from New York came here in 1857 and rented the Union House from Mr. Rice, then opened a shoe shop. He was a good workman and an honest man in every sense of the word. Domestic troubles shortened his useful life and he died mostly of a broken heart, much regretted by all. Mr. Nelson Smith, his son-in-law, was a pleasant, genial citizen; he died soon after Mr. Hopkins.

Mr. Hogle kept a grocery these times, and was quite useful in the church and society. The Forneys came later, in 1858, we believe, and have added much to the energy of our city.

Jerry, the inimitable caterer for the public tables of our citizens, who never had an enemy but plenty of friends, must not be overlooked in this connection, for he is too closely identified in the history of feasting and dancing—of wassail and song. He also had a harness shop some years ago, and now is in an extensive produce business.

Mr. Webster, in the summer of 1856, sold a great

many lots and laid the foundation of his large fortune during that time. Marshalltown had, perhaps, the greatest accession of population this year than any other year in her history, excepting since the war. The next year, Mr. William Smith, an Englishman, laid out quite a garden and nursery, to supply the town with vegetables and fruit.

New comers were welcomed then, for every one counted against Marietta, so Miles Rice is reported to have said. There was no gradation yet in social rank; all were neighbors, friends. Mrs. J. M. Sherwood brought the first piano to the village, which epoch was marked by a profound sensation.

Mr. John Utz came in 1856; had a grocery, one of the best in the place. He was a prominent member of the Lutheran church. Mr. Utz is now at the head of one of the finest marble manufacturing establishments in the West. His monument to the lamented Deloss is a splendid affair, made of the purest Italian marble, and will cost nearly a thousand dollars.

In 1858 came Mr. George Weille from Illinois, and while waiting for the roads to get better to continue a journey, was induced to remain in the new town and opened the first jewelry store. Since that time, in company with Messrs. Gettings, Beckwith and others, he went to Colorado and amassed a splendid fortune in mining claims, buildings, etc. Mr. Weille and his charming wife who came from merrie England, will be sadly missed as they go to their mountain home across the Nebraska.

As one strolled down Main street in the summer of 1858, he would not see all the faces then that we study there now. Many have emigrated to Colorado and other mining countries, the war took the bravest and the best, while a few, careworn and furrowed, yet plod on in the treadmill of business. Mr. William Bremmer who divided the honors of County Surveyor with Thomas Mercer, Esq., of Marietta, is one of these

9

last mentioned.   He is still seen with his compass and
chain in our streets.

HON. H. C. HENDERSON,

Who ably represented this county in the State Senate
for two sessions of the legislature, came also about
this time.   Mr. Henderson is a brother to Brig. Gen.
Henderson of Knox county, Illinois; is of good stock,
and has been connected with so many public enterprises of the county, that his history is intimately
interwoven with it.   The Methodist Episcopal church,
the temperance reform, all benevolent and Christian
charities, are indebted to Mr. Henderson for a ready
assistance.   He is a lawyer of great ability, ofttimes eloquent, but is generally sought after in counsel, because
of his spotless reputation as to honesty, etc.

Mr. Calvin W. Taft, now the owner of the splendid
nursery started by Mr. Woodbury, came earlier, in the
summer of 1854.   Mr. Taft brought from the Western
Reserve, (the land of cheese-tubs and abolitionists)
that earnest love of freedom which characterizes the
Buckeye Yankees.   Mr. T. was Justice before Mr.
Yeamans, who, by the way, made an excellent officer
both in church and state.

Perry C. Holcomb also came from the Reserve and
owned the first hardware store, in the building now
occupied by M. Rosenbaum.   Mr. Holcomb was young
then, and has established a good business, is quite
wealthy, and with his agreeable wife, is found among
the *elite* of the city.

Mr. E. Brooks, our capable and efficient chief
marshal on public occasions, came in 1856, if we
mistake not.   He is a graceful equestrian for a man of
his years.   We wish we had space for a more lengthened sketch of the old settlers.

H. ANSON. ESQ.　　　　Dʳ GEORGE GLICK.

COL SHURTZ.
8ᵀᴴ CAV.

HON. G. M. WOODBURY.　　　　T. B. ABELL. ESQ.

HON. G. M. WOODBURY

Came to Marshalltown in 1854, from Peoria, Illinois, and moved into an old building now occupied by Rev. Mr. Dunton, although it has been completely renovated since. This house had but two rooms; there were no lumber or shingles to be got, so Mr. Woodbury put on a cloth roof. Mr. Pratt and family coming into the town, and having no house, it was arranged that they should take one of the rooms, leaving small quarters for either household.

A pleasing incident occurred soon after their arrival at their new home. So many settlers coming in, the supply of provisions was less than the demand, but some enterprising farmer below, had brought in a wagon load of slaughtered hogs; Mr. Woodbury bought three, but on bringing them home, where should he put them? He was in a worse quandary than the man who bought the elephant! no cellar, woodshed, meat-house or barn. Finally, Mrs. W. proposed the old joiner's bench that lay out of doors— place them in it, heads and points, and cover with the wagon sheet, which all emigrants had at the time. Often in the winter, the wolves would come in the night for a snack, notwithstanding the formidable whizzing of an old rifle that Frederick and John (sons of Mr. Woodbury) kept standing by the bed-post. When the family wanted meat, they were obliged to whack off with an ax the frozen slices.

John Woodbury made the model, about one foot in length, of the first steam engine ever made in the Iowa valley, working industriously under the canvas roof, with such light only as came through the cloth. He should have taken place beside Watt and other youthful geniuses who have wrought like the Cyclops of old, to forge thunderbolts in solitude and alone. But we wish, more particularly, to speak of his honored father, who has done more than any other man to develop the resources of Marshall County, and, in fact, for a long way up the Iowa valley. He built the first grist mill, just north of Marshalltown; the people being obliged to go to Cedar Rapids or Oskaloosa to mill, and when we consider the dreadful condition of the roads in early times, we may appreciate something of the favor that was conferred on the inhabitants by the establishment of this enterprise. Any failure of the "grist" brought corn boiled in the grain for bread, or else pounded in a mortar for that purpose. He afterwards built mills at Xenia and Alden on the Iowa river, just over the Hardin line, and sold flour to grocers and others "on tick," supplying the whole northwestern part of the State for some years. On his rounds for collection of these flour bills and other business, he relates a funny scene in which his lady and himself were actors. Mrs. Woodbury accompanied him through a trip, and on coming to Owl Lake, in Wright county, they found a slough that looked dubious, but Mr. W. thought it could be crossed without much trouble. He had a single horse and buggy; after going a little way, down went the horse and vehicle into the mud and water. Here was a fix, no passing team, no house within five or six miles. Pretty soon Mr. W. succeeded in getting the horse unharnessed, and as every one knows, he never turns *back*ward, in due time the animal found himself on firm ground in the right direction. Next, the baggage was landed safely on the other side. Mr. Woodbury having removed his coat and boots, was by this time in good working condition. Then, how to get the wife across! Finally, after much coaxing she was carried over, papoose fashion, upon the broad shoulders of her doughty knight, and then to crown the afternoon's work, he placed himself between the shafts of the buggy and drew it across in triumph, pretty well exhausted by that time.

But, perhaps, with the court house enterprise, Mr. W. showed as much backbone as anywhere in his career. After the election of 1856 it was thought best to build a town hall, with vaults, jury box, and county offices, so that if " *the* majority " could be prevailed upon to vote for Marshalltown as the county seat, everything would be ready for occupancy, and call it a court house. Every citizen of the village was asked to help; some gave but ten dollars and that in work. The financial crash of 1857 coming on made matters worse. But the pertinacious " never-give-up" Mr. Woodbury, with Rice, Dr. Glick and Anson, kept to work, rolled up their sleeves, and used the hammer and saw with the workmen. Borrowing eight hundred dollars of the Methodist Episcopal Church, and with their subscription paper, they soon had the building on its foundations before Marietta was aware of the project. And when the farmers came into town to trade, many helped tend mason a little time, or drew a load of brick, etc.

How handsomely the voters of the right stripe were treated ! Many a calico dress, and packages of tobacco, dried apples, and tea, found their way into the homes of the faithful—to Marshalltown.

When the summer swallows came to build their nests in the May-time of 1858 the eaves were ready, and the temple of Justice lifted its portals for the Court to enter at its May term, Judge Thompson presiding, had the majesty of the law been maintained by Marietta.

But it was mainly in connection with the early extension of the Cedar Rapids Railroad that Marshall County has great need of gratitude to Mr. Woodbury. It was due to his energy and the liberality of our citizens, that the line was extended so near the city, and came to such rapid completion after the project was talked of by capitalists. At the time of the preliminary survey, he raised a subscription (to carry forward the enterprise) of seven hundred dollars, some of which was given in sums of twenty-five cents. It was the widow's mite, for many were poor but extremely anxious the road should be built. Some would have scorned the help of twenty-five cent men — not so Mr. Woodbury. The survey was made, and he was elected vice-president and director of the road, and held these important offices for four years, when he resigned after seeing the line built through the county.

Mr. Woodbury donated freely for a survey of the Marshalltown, Newton and Pella Railroad, to be built through the Chicauqua and Iowa "divides," but the project has not met with success. Not only in railroads, banks, mills, and factories, but in the beneficent charities of the day, we honor the subject of this sketch.

Mr. W. was elected one of the early trustees of the Orphans' Home, and through his influence we had the credit of the State Fair in 1865. The churches of Marshalltown have all received tokens of his generosity, and in many instances the lowly and destitute have appealed to his aid and he has not been slow in response.

About the time of finishing the court house, the enterprise called into existence the first organization of ladies, governed by their own officers, and named

THE BELL SOCIETY.

They met afternoons at private houses, and had a good time with their sewing and chit-chat. Mrs. S. Lacy was elected president, Mrs. Chester Heald, secretary, Mrs. P. C. Holcomb, treasurer, and Mrs. Lizzie Smith, corresponding secretary. We suppose the latter office was filled for the purpose of obtaining a bell by correspondence, at Troy, or some other place where they were manufactured. Mrs. Smith says, however, the correspondence connected with the Society, was not very "lofty."

We hear of a little gossip from their chatting, that has floated down from the past, which we will write down for them to laugh over to-day. One of their number had been raised in Baltimore and not being *acquainted* with garden truck in its normal condition, took a hoe and went out to get some cucumbers. She returned to the house where she was boarding, and reported a woful lack of cucumbers, for she had dug up three hills and could not find a single one! She supposed they grew like potatoes!

The members of this society paid five dollars fine if the hostess had more than one kind of cake or fruit for supper. Quite a premium on hospitality in those days.

At one of the literary societies which had an existence about this time, Mrs. Lacy read an essay on the prospects of the growing city. She also avowed the purpose of the ladies to help finish the court house in time for the election, that is, they would use hammer and nails, planes and saws, upon the temple of Justice. It was Juno nerving Eurystheus to difficult labors. Mr. Woodbury took them at their word, and ordered them out on Monday to take their places with the volunteer workmen. We are painfully conscious of Mr. Woodbury's want of sagacity, which has always marked his career, with this exception. Had he named any other day but Monday, the ladies would have generously responded to the call, for the ladies then did not scruple to overlook the wash-tub. The result was, but a few *responded*. After this, when the public square was to be fenced, they enclosed three sides, buying all the lumber, nails, etc.; and in carrying on their enterprises, they had

TAMBOS,

As they were called by a Marshall lady through some inadvertence of memory. "Tambos!" "Tambos!" she repeated, "Are they good to eat?" Many had never seen tableaux and knew nothing of scenic effect, and pious people in the churches talked of the rigors of discipline if they were repeated, denouncing them as an incipient theatre. A large fund was raised from the entertainment, and it passed off pleasantly to all concerned. An incident occurred just before the performance began. Mr. Wasson in arranging the curtains was behind them, and a light showed him full length, with his hair sticking up as if in need of a pair of shears. "Tambos, Number 1," whispered Pete Hepburn to a lady; as the head kept bobbing from side to side like a jumping jack, the candles being in just the right position to make a really laughable scene Mr. Wasson, now one of our dignified merchants and a perfect gentleman, perhaps may have forgotten his role in the performance.

In 1858, came Mr. M. Rosenbaum, one of our foremost business men, and an excellent critic in literature and art, and with his intelligent lady made quite an addition to the circle of friendly intercourse and enjoyment. He was from Mansfield, Ohio. His wife died a few years ago, and he has since married a lady from the sunny South, of most agreeable manner and charming ways.

We must not overlook a brave soldier, that served three years in the army, and has done what he could for the Church—Mr. A. L. Vertz. He married a step-daughter of Mr. John Smith, who was quite an old settler, and lived on the Taft place, as it is now called. He is Judge Smith's father, and came here about 1852.

In the fall of 1859, the market for grain was so depressed—corn worth only ten cents per bushel—

that Mr. Woodbury concluded to start a distillery to relieve the farmers. In October, he sent to Dubuque, by Mr. G. Hartwell, his engineer and master workman, for his castings. On reaching Union Grove, near the northeast corner of the county, he slipped accidentally under his wagon which was heavily loaded with flour, and was fatally injured, so that he died in a day or two after the occurrence. He left a widow with six little children to buffet with western life. But admirably Mrs. H. has performed her duties, as every citizen can testify. Mr. Woodbury only kept the distillery in operation about a year, we are glad to record, and there has never been another here.

METHODIST EPISCOPAL CHURCH.

The pioneer church planted her standards early in the county, and the itinerant was seen with his Bible and saddle-bags, soon after the sound of the swinging ax and hum of bees marked the presence of the hardy emigrant. In 1851, Rev. Mr. Corkhill, and Rev. S. Dunton, familiarly called Father Dunton, occupied the Iowa City pulpit, but being aware of the needs of Central Iowa for missionary work, Father Dunton was persuaded to undertake the enterprise of founding the Marshall Mission. Late one night he reached a cabin on Linn Creek occupied by Mr. Ralls, chilled and hungry by his long ride. After enjoying Mr. R.'s hospitality, he attempted to go onward to Marietta, but after traveling perhaps twenty miles and trying to cross the creek, the high water having swung the only bridge from its position, he was obliged to return to Iowa City until a more favorable opportunity. Late in the spring he came back and organized a class or rather the first church in Marshall county, at the Mr. Griffiths we have already mentioned, at the corner of Le Grand. We think there were ten persons in the class. Afterward, about 1853, he organized another

10

class, in Marshalltown, at the school-room in a house owned by Christopher Ford, and when the infant church was moved into the frame school-house, now used as the primary department of the public school, it fell under the care of Rev. Mr. Armstrong. But its progress was slow, and in the spring of 1857 it numbered only thirty members. Alas! too many associate their worship with the splendid frescoes, the rich music of the organ, the eloquent tones of the preacher, forgetting that He is near, even in the small crowded room with rude pulpit and benches; yet the early Methodists had nothing of this. It was for a later age to find out that there is an aristocracy among the followers of the humble carpenter and fishermen of Galilee; that to turn up their noses at the representatives of these humble trades, is better than to wash the disciples' feet at His command. How Barbara Heck and Mrs. Fletcher would sigh to walk up the aisles of some of our fashionable churches!

But we return to the days of Rev. Mr. Stewart, and the quaint, yet forcible Br. Shinn, who was once appointed temporary chaplain of the House of Representatives. We insert the prayer upon that occasion. "Great God, bless the young and growing State of Iowa, bless her senators and representatives, bless her State officers, give us a sound currency, pure water, and undefiled religion, for Christ's sake. Amen."

Then we hear of Rev. Mr. Babcock in 1859; afterward Rev. L. Truesdall who went in 1861 as Chaplain to the Second Iowa Cavalry. At the time of his pastorate there was a great deal of dissension and bitter feeling, many were suspended, and it was an hour of deep gloom. The town had borrowed their building fund, so it was necessary to meet in the court house, the school room being too small. The Upper Iowa Conference met there in 1861, Bishop Scott presiding, who always seemed to us a representative of St. John, so sweet and mild is he in his manner to the brethren.

In this conference year, the pastoral mantle fell upon
Rev. Mr. Fuller, a popular preacher, and Rev. J. Rankin was presiding elder. In September, 1862, Rev.
Mr. Thompson was appointed for a year, and the
church very slowly made headway against the hosts
of darkness, and not till the second year of the good
Br. Rankin as pastor, did the noble old church come
from under the cloud, " fair as the sun, clear as the
moon, and terrible as an army with banners."

They, at this time, finished and furnished the chapel
commenced in 1861, and since, under the ministrations
of Rev. Mr. Kendig, and the gifted, scholarly Prof.
Fellows, the church has taken her place in the front
of the battle, having a good choir and organ, a membership of 180, pays a salary of $1,200 per annum to
the clergyman, besides donating largely to charitable
objects. There is a Dorcas Society connected with the
church, Mrs. M. A. Boardman, president, and Miss M.
Hickox, secretary.

CAMP MEETING.

The first camp fires ever built by the Marshall Mission flamed through the forest near Griffith's mill on
Timber creek. Here, with no rustling silks or "jew-
els' shine," the old-fashioned Methodists from far and
near, met in prayer and praise, Father Dunton took the
lead and with another worthy brother carried on a
very good work, with nothing to mar their sweet enjoyment of Christian love and duty.

The Methodist Episcopal Church in Marshall county
has a membership of nearly eight hundred, five cir-
cuits with efficient pastors, and a parochial care of
Sabbath Schools and "classes" at different points.
Rev. J. S. Edwards, a young local preacher of great
revival influence, has organized several classes and
does glorious work in the vineyard of the Lord.

A NEW SCHOOL PRESBYTERIAN CHURCH

Was organized in 1858, and met in the court house, with Rev. N. Gordon as pastor. There was a little handful of the members—only nine. Mrs. Gerhart, a member of the Dutch Reformed Church, gave in her letter to make the number ecclesiastically complete. Mr. Gordon was a good man, right on the essential question of slavery which then agitated all religious bodies, but was not popular as a sensation preacher, and he remained only a year or so. Mr. John Fisher and N. Gillespie were the first deacons. After Mr. Gordon left, President Geiger of the Albion College preached occasionally, until 1862, when Rev. Mr. Deloss came to the town on a visit, and was prevailed upon to remain and minister to the wants of the church. And nobly he responded to the call, urged a closer union in spiritual matters, and the erection of a church structure ; he then appealed to every citizen of Marshalltown to give something to help lay its foundation and build thereon. He succeeded admirably, and the result was, that this church has one of the finest edifices in the State. Beautifully frescoed and painted, warmed by furnaces and lit by splendid chandeliers, a good organ and choir, and a flourishing Sabbath School, with only a small debt to detract from its financial success.

Mr. and Mrs. Gettings were among its first members, and still mingle with a large and fashionable congregation. Mrs. Gerhart is not living. Mr. Deloss did not live to see the end of his great work, and after a long and painful illness, just as the sun was tinting with its evening glories the spires and roof of his loved church, he sank to rest, praying sadly and sweet, " Thy will be done."

We never shall forget his masterly effort at the death of the martyred Lincoln ; the pure diction, the forcible language, all told the orator, the patriot and the Christian. It was nearly his last public effort; worn down with anxieties for the church and nation, his vigorous nature sank under it, and he sleeps in the cemetery that he was mainly instrumental in beautifying and ornamenting as befitting a burial place for the dead in our midst. The church is now under the pastoral care of Rev. Mr. Kellogg, a man ably fitted to fill the place of the lamented Deloss. The church building was commenced in 1863 and finished in 1865.

LUTHERAN CHURCH.

We may state that this organization is connected with that of Albion, generally, alternating public service with them. Prof. Geiger preached here, also the eloquent Schaeffer, the Rev. Messrs. Sternberg and Fair, and latterly the very classical Rev. W. Lepley. Their church building was commenced in 1861, the first in the city, but was not finished until 1864. It saw a deal of financial trouble, but by the united effort of Mr. Schaeffer and people it was nearly cleared from debt at its dedication in January, 1865. It saw great prosperity while under his guidance, but dissensions creeping in very stealthily at first, they are now without pastor or choir, and have rented their beautiful church to the

BAPTISTS,

Who were organized here in 1863 with sixteen members, meeting for worship at the court house, and Woodbury's Hall. Rev. Mr. Willy first, then Rev. N. Holmes from Webster City, have been the pastors of this church. They have a membership of over seventy, a splendid edifice in process of erection, which will be finished the coming season, and a Sabbath School of sixty scholars.

DISCIPLES CHURCH,

Sometimes called the Campbellite Baptists, have been holding meetings for two years in the court house, Rev. M. W. McCondell, pastor.

Their Sabbath School numbers fifty pupils, and the membership is constantly increasing in numbers and influence.

UNIVERSALISTS.

Claiming for their peculiar tenets the broad and liberal idea of the Fatherhood of God and brother-hood of man, and a practical christianity—theirs is the oldest church in the city. They have no place of worship, excepting in the town hall of Mr. Wood-bury, but have purchased a lot and intend to build soon. Their minister, Rev. J. P. Sanford, who has just returned from a journey to the Holy Land, with sandals wet by the sacred waters of the Jordan, will be a power to help them in the erection of a suitable church edifice for the wants of a large and wealthy organization.

MITE SOCIETIES, ETC.

Every church in the city has the above connected with them, mostly sustained by the energies of the ladies, the proceeds being used as a contingent fund. The meetings of these societies are very pleasant and agreeable, especially to strangers, as we have many coming in.

The Masons number about ninety. Odd Fellows, sixty-five, and the Good Templars, now battling against the enemy under the third organization, have a membership of seventy-five, with Mr. J. Roe as W. C.

THE PRESS.

As we have already mentioned the incidents con-nected with the establishing of the press at Albion and

Marietta, making obeisance to Prof. Wilson as the senior editor, we take up the thread of history where the Iowa Central was removed to Marshalltown, appearing under the name of the Marshall County Times, with Hon. H. C. Henderson and Dr. Taylor as editors. This was in 1860. In the summer of 1862, Chapin & Co. bought the old Marietta Express office, and published, in Mr. John Fisher's block, a journal under the name of the Iowa Valley News. This office burned down at the time of the great fire in the building. Previous to this, Mr. R. H. Barnhart being the publisher of the Times, sold out to Mr. W. H. Gallup, who appeared as both editor and publisher. After the fire. Messrs. Chapin & Co. bought out the aforesaid Times, and with the remnant of his last enterprise, started out like the fabled Phœnix into the sunshine of popular favor under the name of the Marshall County Times and News, in 1863.

In connection with this weekly, Judge Ed. Rice started a daily, but after three months of existence it died out.

Messrs. Carlton and Howard, partners of Chapin, went into the army in Capt. Woodbury's Company, leaving the *Chapin* to go on alone without the *Co.*

In the summer of 1864, Barnhart Bros. established the Marshall County Expositor, a democratic paper, which was published with a moderate degree of success through a period of a year and six months.

Mr. Gallup repurchased the Times office, but in a short time sold to J. J. Britton, Esq., of Springfield, Ill., who again sold the unlucky elephant after an ownership of seven weeks and sinking over three hundred dollars, having bought both Times and Expositor offices, and published under the name of the Marshalltown Union.

The irrepressible Chapin came to Mr. Britton's rescue, taking the place of Prof. T. Clarke upon the tripod, who went to Chicago and was afterward known as the

author of " Sir Copp." Chapin associated with him
George Barnhart; the firm soon doubled the subscription list of the re-baptized Times, and in the summer
of 1865, they sold to H. C. Henderson, and after a
year of successful management, the office passed into
the hands of C. Aldrich, Esq. and H. Welsh of Webster City, and the Times waves its banners still tri-
umphant, with the largest circulation of any county
paper in the State.

Messrs. Gregg (our senior lawyer), and Carlton, are
publishing a neat reliable democratic journal, on the
north side of the public square, yclept the Marshall
County Advance—an excellent local sheet.

HORTICULTURAL SOCIETY.

This organization is of recent date, but embraces
some of the most influential citizens in the county.
Hon. Thomas Mercer is president, and Hon. E. H.
Chapin, secretary. Messrs. Woodbury and Aldrich
have offered magnificent premiums in connection with
this society.

There is also a Young Men's Christian Association
in progress, with Hon. H. W. Henderson as president,
and J. A. Mabie, secretary.

A fine debating club is in existence, whereof Mr.
Ed. Boardman is the presiding officer, we believe.
There is, too, a literary association with Prof. Wilson
at its head, that has been of great benefit to the citizens of Marshalltown in introducing citizens from
abroad, and in discussions of the questions that
agitate society, they have been ably met by the
members.

AID SOCIETIES.

After the war broke out and the soldiers needed
sanitary supplies, there was a society organized in
October, 1861, to aid the brave " boys in blue."

Mrs. M. Rosenbaum was chosen president, and Miss Sarah Jane Howell, secretary. This was kept up under different officers for several years and was rather merged into the Orphans' Home Fair Society that was organized in May, 1865. This is so recent we have no space for its whole history, and will just note, that there was a great deal of hard work done, and all wrought as much as they were able. Perhaps the costliest present that any one lady gave, was the silk bed quilt presented by Mrs. J. M. Sherwood, which netted one hundred and thirty dollars. The whole proceeds of the Orphans' Home Fair at Marshalltown was sixteen thousand dollars.

As the years rolled on, almost every enterprise here has received an impetus from the white hand of woman. In aiding churches, schools, fairs, and the different societies for the freedmen and soldiers, she has borne an honorable part. Much of the labor of Sabbath Schools is performed by the ladies in getting up entertainments, fairs, etc., for their benefit. There are over thirty schools in the county, and that of the Methodist Episcopal Church, in Marshalltown, being the largest, numbers over two hundred and fifty pupils. It is supposed that there are nearly a thousand children in the Sabbath Schools of Marshall county.

CELEBRATION OF CEDAR RAPIDS AND MISSOURI RAIL-
ROAD.

In March, 1863, the track being finished to Marshall-town, her citizens proposed to entertain the world, and Chicago in particular, to the best they had for good cheer, and with unbounded hospitality. There was a grand supper at Woodbury's Hall, toasts were drank, speeches made, and all were brim full of hilarity and joy at the completion of the line. Among other things said, the Hon. H. C. Henderson reported, "that the cattle along the line had grown fat since the road was

built, the ladies were prettier, and the corn had promised to 'grow one hundred bushels to the acre' the
coming season.' "

The Chicago representatives seemed delighted with
the attentions paid them, and they returned the com-
pliment by giving our citizens the freedom of the
Garden City in a great measure.

The following poem, composed and sung by Prof.
Heighton, was an interesting feature of the celebration:

> Hurrah! for the age of progression,
>   Of telegraphs, printing and steam,
> Success to each lawful profession,
>   Especially those worked by steam.
>
> *   *   *   *
>
> There's a price for the old farmer's turnips,
>   A smile in his truth-beaming eye
> As he bids you a welcome "good morning,"
>   For he knows that the station is nigh.
>
> The merchant, the priest and mechanic,
>   The doctor and lawyer, also;
> Each walks, thinks, and acts much faster,
>   For the engine has got them in tow.
>
> Then join the bounding chorus,
>   And let the echo be:
> The anvil, plow and engine—
>   The friends of liberty.

It was a source of gratification to all concerned
that the pioneer road of Central Iowa was so soon to
be finished, for it gave a great impetus to trade, as it
was many miles in advance of any other line in the
State towards the Missouri. Mr. Woodbury, Dr.
Glick, Mr. W. Rice and H. Anson, with other prominent citizens, some who had given twenty-five cent
subscriptions, all met in joyful conclave at the completion of the enterprise.

In the matter of celebrations, we take leave of the
subject, by saying that our citizens were as happy as

any in the republic at the taking of Richmond. Dr. Glick remarked, " I am full of glory ;" Chapin said, " My heart is too full for utterance ;" and the lamented Deloss made one of the most eloquent speeches ever delivered in Marshall county. The whole town was on the sidewalk, congratulating each other—flags blossomed on every sign-post, and at the eaves of mansion and hut; and to have a friend in the army or wearing the " blue" at home, was a matter of deep joy and gratitude.

A PILGRIMAGE

From the Iowa river to the sacred Jordan, with all the fatigues, anxieties, and dangers from storms, Bedouins, and Italian banditti, has been successfully accomplished by the Rev. J. P. Sanford of Marshalltown, the Universalist clergyman ; he also made a visit to the pyramids, and the sites of the ancient Thebes and Memphis of Egypt.

On the 16th and 17th of May, 1867, the " Holy Palmer" as he would have been termed in the days of the crusades, gave to the citizens of Marshalltown his impressions of Europe and Asia, which he traveled over, and the incidents of his journey to the interesting and sacred spots where the world's grandest history has been enacted. The tour was performed in the short space of one hundred and twenty-five days. The lectures were a rare treat to all present, as Mr. Sanford has fine descriptive powers, a voice of great flexibility and sweetness, and a genuine enthusiasm consonant with the hallowed theme, when speaking of the Holy Land. Space forbids us to mention all the rare and curious relics which he obtained upon his pilgrimage and exhibited to the audience. We saw antique vases and lamps from the chambers of the pyramids, scarabæs, and shreds of cerements that wrapped the mummies of three thousand years ago ; olive berries and cedar from the hills of Judea, and shells from the shores of blue Galilee, which may have been pressed by the hallowed feet of the dear Christ eighteen centuries since, not forgetting the water from the sacred Jordan, and Dead Sea, which were all genuine, beyond doubt.   We thank Mr. Sanford most devoutly for making this pilgrimage, as a representative of Iowa, to the old world.

A few more incidents connected with the gentleman's career will be interesting to our readers.   Mr. Sanford was born in Seneca, N. Y., in 1832, consequently he is thirty-five years of age.   At the early age of nine, he lost his mother and was " bound out " three years, and upon his father marrying again, his indentures were canceled and he returned to the home-nest.   But there arose " an unpleasantness," he *Nasbyly* remarks, and after a sound thrashing, he seeks his fortune in the West Indies, Mexico, South America and the Southern States.   After years of wandering he places his pilgrim feet upon Iowa soil, studies for the ministry and becomes a beloved pastor of the Universalist Church.   During the war he was made lieutenant, and captain in the Second Iowa Cavalry, also a Colonel in the Forty-Seventh Iowa Infantry.

In the summer of 1865, he traveled over Europe and the British Isles, and in the past winter crossed the Atlantic a second time and visited the Holy Land, Egypt, etc., as we have mentioned.

His lectures have been pronounced by good critics as equal to Taylor's in word-painting and poetic enthusiasm.   He should publish an account of his travels in book form for the benefit of his many friends in Iowa.

The transition from word-painters to artists who paint with sunbeams, is comparatively easy as we gossip of our goodly citizens.

Mr. Datesman was the first artist in Marshalltown claiming from Daguerre the principles of the art so mysterious to the early pioneers, long before the age of ambrotype, photograph, etc. What wonderful improvements we see in the pictures of to-day and those of twelve years ago. He was not the pioneer artist of the county, that honor being worn by F. Baum, who in Marietta made life-scenes from the bronzed features of the old settlers in 1854, a year before the advent of P. Datesman in Marshalltown.

Mr. Baum has published a beautiful map of Marshall county, giving to all a fine delineation of the different groves, water- and section-lines of the townships. They are now associated together in art-work and do a good business in their gallery on Main street, only equaled by the Hoosier soldier, J. Lee Knight, he taking the premium at the county fair of 1865 for the finest photographs on exhibition.

We have also an artist of real genius in the lithe, graceful figure of Miss C. A. Shaw, who has achieved wonders on canvas without crossing the threshold of any school of design, being entirely self-taught. She has an excellent likeness of Mrs. Giddings, one of our best families, from Ohio, a relative of Hon. Joshua Giddings, "the old man eloquent."

VIENNA.

Vienna township occupies the north-east corner of the county—has grove, water, prairie without stump or stone, ready for the plow-share, and with the advantage of a moral, intelligent people, it is one of the most desirable spots of earth to live upon. The Iowa makes a bend around the south-west corner of the township, Wolf and Dean Creeks are in the north and center, while Nicholson's heads in the south—in fact, running water in every direction for stock. Mr. Hunsden is one of the earliest settlers, and was postmaster, an office he held from its establishment,—a very loyal man, having sent a whole family of sons to the Union army, two of whom were sacrificed, yet,

like the grand old Roman, he regrets them not, so the
country lives and is saved to liberty and freedom.
He has splendid strawberries and currants, and the
latch-string of hospitality hangs on the door in the
fruit season.

Mr. Cleaver, an excellent citizen, is a refugee from
Canada in the time of the revolution of 1838.   He
was a state prisoner at Toronto eight months and
then banished into exile.   His two sons, James and
Kim, served with distinction and valor in the army ;
one of his daughters, the brown-eyed "Jessie," married Prof. Heighton some years ago.   His farmhouse
is a pleasant resort for citizens of Marshalltown in the
warm season, and many remember with pleasure the
hours spent with music and chess, the smiles of welcome from our hostess, and let us add, the most
fragrant cup of coffee in the county.

Mr. Bradbury, also one of the pioneers and an
Englishman from the vicinity of Rochdale, the home
of John Bright, lived here, and after opening up a
new home in the West and beginning fully to appreciate the greatness of American institutions, fell a victim to disease and crossed to the unknown shore,
leaving his family comparatively strangers in the New
World.   There is a rude grave-yard at Wolf Creek
where he was buried, with scarcely a spot of beauty
but the grand old trees.

We protest against the fashion, we Western people
have, of doing everything for the comfort of the living
and leaving our burial places without a flower to mark
our affection, or sometimes a respectable fence.   We
place the marble there, perhaps, but we ought to cultivate
flowers, visit them often, and not be so afraid of the
dear spot that enshrines the remains of the loved and
lost.

Near this rude cemetery lives an English gentleman
by the name of Jones.   He is a very successful
farmer, showing what superior skill can do with our

rich Iowa soil to aid the agriculturist. His wife is a very pleasant hostess and the family is highly respected in the vicinity.

Mr. Beeman lives near here also—a good man, having a beautiful farm.

With this little digression, we return to the Bradbury family. After the death of her husband, Mrs. Bradbury met with many difficulties, but managed her business in an admirable manner. Her daughter coming from England, was married quite early in life to a Mr. Bowen from New York. This was the largest wedding ever held in Vienna township, but after the hilarities were over, a careless boy on the farm set a straw stack on fire, which caught the barn and burned it with other valuables. It was a great loss, but the neighbors were very kind and helped the family in every possible way.

There is a very thickly settled neighborhood on Wolf creek nearly on the line of Vienna, which holds meetings in the school-house. They have a post office just over the line in Grundy, called Wandaloup, the Latin for wolf, so the schoolmaster said. They are obliged to go twenty miles for a physician or lawyer. If some persons practicing these professions were to settle here, it would save a good deal of travel for Wandaloup.

Mr. Samuel Richey, one of the Board of Supervisors and a very excellent citizen, lives in the southern part of Vienna.

There have been revival meetings held in the school-house near here, under the superintendence of Rev. J. S. Edwards of Marshalltown, and a large class formed of the Methodist Episcopal Church.

Among the prominent citizens of this township we have only space to mention a very few. Mr. Cunningham, Mr. Monlux, Mr. Glass, an old, yet pleasant gentleman, Mr. Walters, and others. We close with a leaf from the tablet of Vienna soldiers.

Mr. David Swartwout left a little family and rallied to his country's call in the Twenty-Third Regiment, but while home on furlough in March, 1864, died there. This was a dreadful stroke to his wife and children, and their son Augustus passed over to the " other shore " from the hospital at New Orleans the next year.

Joseph Vincent, of the rank and file, who carried the old flag at Pea Ridge and was killed on the field, Hiram V. Willey, who laid down his young hopes at Shiloh, and the Hunsden boys who died in hospital, make up the list of the heroic dead. Vienna sent as many men to the army as she cast votes at the previous election—the banner township !

BANGOR TOWNSHIP

Lies in the great highway from Eldora to Marshalltown. Its hills rise from the drowsy Iowa, and the wild bees drone on Honey Creek. One listens to the sweet voices of Quaker girls, and the tinkle of bells in the sheep folds; anon, a hawk circles up from the prairies, and the mists rise from the lowlands, showing the little village of

BANGOR,

With its unpretending churches, its rows of shade trees and cultivated gardens, old fashioned hollyhocks and sunflowers swinging under the windows; doves and darting swallows; the whole picture so suggestive of real comfort, no wonder the poor darkeys when they came from Missouri, exclaimed, " Oh! dis is de happy land of Canaan." At one time there were a good many fugitives about the township, but they have mostly returned to a warmer climate. We have seen a broad-brimmed Ethiopian, of the family of Hagar and Onesimus, occasionally in the streets of Marshalltown, who it seems is a disciple of the rare principles of George Fox.

There were a good many ladies here who were identified with the Soldiers' Aid Society and with the Orphans' Home Fair, who wrought faithfully and well, for they raised over a hundred dollars in this township for the Home.

Among those who were on the Underground Railroad, and a conductor on the same, was Mr. James Owens, now living at Iowa Falls; and Mr. Lounsbury, of Hardin, sometimes gave help. The route was from College Farm, in Jasper county, to Marietta; then taking a team and driving the load onward to Bangor, among some of the good Friends, if not to Mr. Owen's. There were sharp tricks played off upon prying people, and queer disguises used to keep the poor creatures from being taken. How the world *has* moved in seven years!

Mr. Owens went as a missionary among the freedmen through the war, and accomplished a great deal of good among them as well as among the sick soldiers of Iowa regiments.

But yet there is even among the Quakers, a long continued inherent prejudice in favor of the superiority of the Anglo-Saxon. In the Sunday School at Bangor, one of the colored brethren was made a teacher over white children. In spite of the teachings of a hundred years some of the parents remonstrated. Sister Bush, the mother of the teacher, as black as the ace of spades, rose to her feet in the congregation, and forthwith gave the brethren and sisters a severe castigation, as the spirit gave her utterance. She is now in Missouri.

Mr. Lancaster Bell and Mr. N. Lounsbury, also Mr. Owen Albright, are old and time-honored citizens in this region. All have splendidly cultivated farms, and Mr. Albright has the finest fruit in Marshall county. His nursery is in excellent condition; the young trees being thoroughly acclimated, are worth ten times more than importations from the East. We

11

have seen cherries of a delicious flavor and very large size from his garden, that would make the same family of May Dukes blush a deeper red in Ohio. Currants, raspberries, complexioned like Dido, strawberries, and in fact, he raises all the small fruits in great perfection. He was very prominent in building the church at Bangor, and is a good citizen in every capacity. They have a small library and debating club in the village.

Mr. W. W. Weatherly, now land agent in Marshall-town, having been sheriff of the county and a captain in the Marietta war, was, with Dr. Bush, one of the earliest settlers on the Upper Iowa river. His cabin was built not far from Mormon Ridge in the fall of 1850. He relates a melancholy incident connected with a funeral of old Mr. Dean in Marshall township a few months after, in 1851. They had not enough pine lumber to make him a coffin, and were obliged to saw up the sideboards of Mr. Weatherly's wagon to piece out the lid. They were not very poor, but the high water prevented the getting of lumber. It was a time of great trial to Mrs. Dean, but she bravely bore up under all her difficulties.

Civilization, in its irresistible march westward, sometimes seems like a Juggernaut that crushes its victims with less conscience than the Hindoo idol, and the homesick women who pine in emigrant homes are not the least to be pitied.

Mormon Ridge in this township takes its name from the fact that in 1849 a good many of the saints, on their westward march to Salt Lake, were detained here. They dug holes in the hillside for homes, and enlarged their apartments by wagon covers and old quilts. They must have suffered severely from cold, for there are quite a number of graves to be counted in the vicinity.

Coal is seen along the edge of the river not far

from here, and all it needs is a steam pump to remove the water from the shaft, and this valuable mineral could be worked for market.

Mr. Jacob Kinzer has lived in Bangor some years, and is well known as a good citizen and an excellent farmer. There are a number of Carolina Quakers settling in his neighborhood.

The village of Bangor has a pleasant location. There is a store owned by Mr. J. C. Smith of Eldora, formerly of Marshalltown, a blacksmith shop, post-office, etc. Should the railroad ever be built from Eldora to Marshall, Bangor will become an important point, as it is one of the best farming regions of the West. The Methodists and Friends are about equally divided in numbers and influence; the Sabbath Schools are in a flourishing condition.

The first Justice was Mr. Sneldon Wyatt, and his few neighbors at the time, were Mr. Jessup, John Cockett, Silas H. Bentley, and his brothers. Mr. Isaac Miller, who once resided in Marietta, lives here on a good farm, and is a prominent member of the Methodist Episcopal Church. Also a Mr. Cox lives in this vicinity, and Mr. Angus McKinnon, with his brother Lathland —good citizens.

MINERVA.

This township is near the Story line, and tucks its green prairies under it, with here a grove, there a farm house, presenting charming landscapes in the beauty of midsummer. We always fancied this township was named after some good woman, who dispensed her hospitalities upon some intelligent wayfarer—hence the name, for it has creeks of Little and Big Minerva — an improvement on the endless repetition of Washington, Jefferson, etc., to the plague of letter writers and postmasters in the country. Mr. Elder has the honor of being the first settler in this place, having entered his land in 1851. He owned the grove that bears his name, and opened up a good farm at a very early day. He afterwards went to Liberty, and is held in high estimation in this section. Mr. Daniel Stevens, near "Liberty line," was also a pioneer the same year, and Mr. Weatherly, our busy real estate agent now, broke the green sward for his garden and cornfield soon after his arrival. Mr. Weatherly was one of his nearest neighbors, living in Bangor, twelve miles distant.

Mr. Patterson—of military *presence*, both in Mexico and at Marietta—was one of the old settlers. He identified himself with the new township by naming a pretty grove, "Patterson." He is now living in Davenport, and is quite wealthy.

Mr. John Anselme, a Frenchman, was also a pioneer, and soon after there came quite a number of *la belle* countrymen and settled at the little groves and in the best portions of the township. Entering their land, and being careful and industrious, they have become as wealthy farmers as there are in the county. At the time of the Marietta war, French Grove was a good deal excited in favor of the existing capital, and hearing that Dr. Taylor, of Marshalltown, had been connected with the Know Nothing movement, he came very near being lynched by the wrathful citizens as he came into town on business.

There are a few Germans also, who are quite intelligent, and have taken great pains to obtain good school teachers for the past few years.

Mr. Patterson, in 1864, sold his farm and beautiful home to Mr. S. Burkholder, who was an efficient member of the board of supervisors. His house was a great summer resort for the elite of Marshalltown, having pic-nics on his grounds—all being pleasantly entertained by the agreeable hostess and her sister.

The Protestant Methodists have a little church here, which is attended by the community generally.

Among the wealthy farmers, are Mr. George Wantz and Oscar Elliott. But we have not space for a further notice of this township, with the exception of

CLEMENS' CORNERS,

Near the Liberty line, a point well known since 1856, where the first store was built west of Marietta for a good many miles. Mr. Clemens entered the grove which bears his name, and kept a good hotel, whose gleaming fires welcomed the half frozen traveler in the dreadful winter of 1856-7. The mercury fell on the 18th of December, to thirty-six degrees below zero. There is no store now at the " Corners," we believe. The ladies shop in Bangor, Eldora, and in Marshall-town, or around a peddler's wagon.

MARION TOWNSHIP,

Famous in the county war for her defective poll-books, has a very intelligent people, being settled early by Vermont Yankees. There is rich alluvial soil on the bottoms of the Iowa river, also uplands that grow immense corn, so that there is a great variety of land to select from, with plenty of water, timber, etc.

Near the Marshall line lives the family of Mr. Hol-comb who came in 1856 from the Reserve, in Ohio. They had no meat-house or cellar to the cabin, so hanging their smoked shoulders and hams to the eaves, they had a dangling cornice very tantalizing to the wolves, who used to jump upon their hind feet— circus fashion—trying to pull down the meat. Mrs. Holcomb is noted for her splendid dairy.

In the vicinity of Green Mountain lives Mr. Brock, a gentlemanly farmer ; also Mr. Heacocks, and Spencer Day, Esq., who is known in this section for his fine cattle. Mr. G. W. Voorhees was an early settler, and lived near Mr. Holcomb. He had a farm in an early day, and was a relative of the family at Le Grand. He remembers of sending a watermelon as a present to Mr. Holcomb's family by "Jeff," the first year of their pioneer life, which the rascal devoured with the help of a young comrade;—a standing joke upon the aforesaid "Jeff" to this day.

GREEN MOUNTAIN

Was laid out by James Harvey, Esq., one of our most capable business men, and once partner with Dr. Whealen of the Quaker City store. Himself a Vermonter, and his neighbors being mostly from New England, the village soon gave signs of Yankee energy, and there is no doubt that it would have been an important point, had it not been for the financial crash of 1857, which killed the Fulton Air Line Railroad, whose track lay near Green Mountain.

This road received a land grant from Congress of 800,000 acres, and had seventy miles graded, yet it is never heard of now. The grant was transferred to the Cedar Rapids road, and the result was, this village was left out in the cold. Religiously speaking, Green Mountain is Congregational. They have fine school houses in this vicinity, and the country is noted for its beauty, "the prettiest the sun e'er shone on," so an enthusiastic visitor said one summer evening. But we will not pause in this lovely spot, but hurry southward to

FREDONIA,

Another quiet village, that first set its business corners on the track of the Fulton road by the direction of A. J. Cooper, Esq. It found a place upon the maps of Marshall county the same year with its unique, thrifty neighbor, Green Mountain.

Near here is a beautiful church of quite large dimensions, nearly finished, and built of the splendid

stone found in the bed of Rock creek. It presents a
fine appearance and is in every way creditable to that
most singular of all people, the Dunkards. In the
basement they have a cook-house where they roast a
whole ox, and at the feast representing the Lord's
Supper, they have a great variety of dishes prepared
in this apartment. They wash each other's feet in
token of the Master's humility, the priests shave their
crowns but wear the back hair rather long, generally
greeting the disciples with a holy kiss; are a very
devoted people to their peculiar faith. If one of he
church is found guilty of over-reaching in a bargain—
that most wide-spread of all modern sins—he is disci-
plined most rigorously; and if differing from all
other sects in creed, they certainly are a very moral
and quiet people, and set an example for even some of
our orthodox citizens to follow in life-practice. They
have a membership of about one hundred, and are
constantly increasing in numbers. The most of those
in Fredonia came from Ohio, and Rev. Mr. Murray is
their pastor.

In this vicinity, and very well known as a gentlemanly successful farmer, is Mr. John Hughes. He
has excellent buildings for a new country, and everything has a neat business look, as if farming was an
earnest, intelligent occupation.

Mr. James Reed also lives near here, a brother-in-
law of Mr. Joel Brock—very pleasant people, and
whose interest in our county fairs never flags, or in
any other enterprise to develop the resources of Iowa.
Near Fredonia, eastward, lives Dr. Haynes, quite a
successful physician; also in that vicinity, Rev. Mr.
Benn, who ministers in sacred things to a small church
in the village, and at Orford. He is a very useful man.
Mr. Downs, once a citizen of Marshalltown, who did
a heavy business in forwarding, lives not far from
Fredonia.

An Englishman, by the name of Stubbs, lives in this vicinity who is quite wealthy—made it all by his industry and foresight. He has sometimes fifty head of stock for sale on his beautifully cultivated farm. Mr. Samuel Gilkinson, a good citizen and one of the early settlers, lived near here, but has lately moved to Nebraska.

Mr. Cooper had the first store in Fredonia and did a good business for some time, but Marshalltown filling up so rapidly, he sold out to a Mr. Zearing, and is now our Recorder—a very faithful officer and a worthy man.

But farther back, in the "age of wolves," as an old pioneer facetiously terms it, lived Mr. Alexander Bowles, who came about 1849. They were at one time without game even, being out of ammunition, and were obliged to make soup of deer hides, without a mouthful of anything else. They parched corn and wheat, and ground it in a common coffee-mill for bread, sometimes boiling the grain whole in the kernel. As near as can be ascertained, this family suffered as much as any in the Iowa valley. Mr. Bowles has always been a great hunter, a perfect Nimrod among the wolves and prairie chicks, and partly sustained his family in this manner for many years. Of course they lived in a cabin, hunted, fished, and raised what they could, till the era of sulky-plows and corn-planters. Mr. Samuel Deter's home may be seen not far from Mr. Bowles', and he is a very reliable, honest man. His sons follow in his footsteps, and are cultivating good farms in this section.

Broom corn, sorghum, potatoes, and everything that grows out of doors in Iowa, wave in the sunlight of Marion township.

GREENCASTLE.

Greencastle township is situated in the southeastern part of the county, the Marshalltown and Grinnell road passing through it. It is finely watered by tributaries of Timber creek and North Skunk, and has excellent farming land, with a good deal of timber in the northern portion. There are many sheep and very fair stock owned in Greencastle, and it is in every way a desirable portion of the Hawkeye heritage to emigrants, with the single exception of church privileges, as they have preaching only fortnightly in this township, this being mainly due to the exertions of the Christian Church. Judge Smith is now a resident here, and preaches occasionally. With the help of co-laborers, much good has been done; the Methodists also have a fair representation.

Elias Hilsabeck is the oldest settler here, having come from Illinois in 1852 and entered his land. He is a very worthy farmer and a good citizen. Mr. Lantis, who formerly lived in Timber Creek township, is now a resident of Greencastle. His son, a very brave young man, died in the Union army. Mr. L. tried living in Missouri, but came back to Iowa perfectly contented with the magnificent land of the Musquaquas. The water is so much superior to that State, that this feature of our county will always make it an object to settlers.

Mr. Hoes, formerly of Marshalltown, with "his sheep and cattle upon a thousand hills," lives in Greencastle; also Mr. Dwight of the same place, is now tilling land instead of broom making; he was the first to furnish these useful articles to the citizens of Marshalltown.

Captain Haskins of the "Old Thirteenth" is a citizen of this township, and in his bachelor home surrounded by luxuries, has no desire to return to the battle-field.

12

In looking over the map, we find the site of Green-castle village, which once had the aspiration to be another New York, and if it could buy up some of the votes in this portion of the Hawkeye State, might be a county seat, in case Marietta and Marshalltown should eat each other up, like the giants in the fable. Mr. Blakely Brush was the chief Rajah of this town, and built a large two-story house without wings, which always bore the name of "the Castle." A few years since, Mr. Akers bought the dilapidated fortress, filled the loop holes with glass instead of old coats, and righted up the chimney tops and fence, and it now makes a very respectable appearance.

It was at Justice S. Haskins, just over the line of Le Grand, that Attorney Hepburn and Hon. T. Brown had their little prize-ring exercise. Some years ago, a ditty ran thus, the only thing on record which commemorates the event:

> Ah! Peter, Peter!
> Pumpkin eater!
> How could you thus strike down,
> Or pull the hair
> And scratch the eyes
> Of Honorable Timothy Brown?

But these gentlemen have risen to such high positions in life they may have forgotten this episode of the law.

One cool day in October, 1854, Mr. Jonathan Reed, of Ohio, left his wife and family in the wagon, out on the sea of brown grass, about three miles from any neighbor, sewing a tent cover, while he started to Oskaloosa for flour. After a good deal of stitching and the tent pins being drove into the ground, it was found that by no manner of means would the cover fit upon them, managed by unskillful hands. The boys thought they could build a turf house, but night came on before the abode was but a little way above the foundations. Finally, after a night in the wagon on a lonely prairie, and becoming discouraged with the turf, it was concluded to go back to Mr. Hilsabeck's smoke-house and live in that until Mr. Reed should return and a house could be built. Mr. R. came back in about a week, and a small house was erected that fall, after three or four weeks sojourn in the smoke-house. Mr. Reed has been prominent in the county, filling offices of trust, and is a man of unflinching principle and integrity. He has fine taste in horses, and owns some excellent animals. We have tested the hospitality of this family, after Mr. Reed sold, and went to Le Grand, and know that it was a charming place to spend an hour.

Mr. Clogston, and Mr. John H. Seiger, have made Greencastle their home, and we believe there is no better township in the county. About sixty families live here.

EDEN

Is situated in the extreme southwestern portion of the county. Perhaps, there is not a better township of land in Iowa than Eden, often called by its happy soubriquet, "Paradise." Watered by Clear creek and its tributaries, also by the head springs of North Skunk, with large groves of the best timber for many miles, and noted truthfully for the beautiful "lay of the land"— like a picture. This soil is of unusual depth and fertility; one particular field owned by Greene Allen has been farmed for eighteen seasons without any percep- tible diminution of the crop when properly cultivated. Protected by the groves, wild and tame fruits reach great perfection; the fences are of the most substantial character, barns and out-houses likewise, everything cosy and thrifty about the farms, denoting wealth and prosperity.

EDENVILLE.

This village is contemporaneous with Fredonia and Green Mountain, having been laid out by C. B. Rhodes, Esq., in 1856, and now contains two hotels, a store, two blacksmith shops, a large flouring mill, cabinet shop, and a large school-house used for church purposes. There is an organization of Disciples, but the Methodists are the most numerous—have a parsonage neatly fitted up for Rev. Mr. Bolton, and it is hoped they will carry out the project of building a church edifice the present season. The earliest settler in the vicinity was Greene Allen, who came upon his claim of six hundred acres in 1849. No fear of Indians, prairie fires, wolves, bears, etc., deterred him from his improvements; when the troubles arose on Timber creek he would not go into the fort but kept the even tenor of his way. He has lately returned from a sojourn of six years in Oregon.

A man by the name of Maggard lived in a cabin near Clear creek, and made a little improvement, but taking a fever from exposure, died before there were a half-dozen families within twenty miles to mourn for the pioneer.

Among the earliest settlers was Rev. Thomas Mendenhall, a Protestant clergyman, still living in Edenville; and Rev. Simon Woolston, who labored faithfully in the church, for temperance, and also for Masonry, and is still carrying on these good works in Missouri. He had a large family of sons and daughters who settled here, comprising some of the most influential citizens in the township.

Mr. Owen and Simon Price came about the same time, and Mr. Andrew Logan, who published the first newspaper in Iowa, at Davenport, in 1836. He still survives an amiable wife who is buried not far from the mill in the village grave-yard where too sleeps Mrs. M. Rhodes, the victim of a terrible accident by fire.

This grave-yard needs attention from loving hands, for there are not even rail pens to enclose all the graves, in the Iowa fashion. The grave-yard in the north part of the town is not much better as to embellishment.

Near here lives Mr. P. A. Culver, alternating with Mr. C. Rhodes in the honors of township supervisor, and a man of upright life and principle. Mr. Tuffree from Pittsburg, Pa., came to Eden in 1855, fenced his land and built his house when the wolves howled anything but a welcome to the hardy settler. Mr. Rutson Bullock came later, also Mr. Jeroleman who from small means has become quite wealthy and takes many premiums at the county fairs for good stock. Mr. Bullock keeps an excellent hotel at State Center, also Mr. A. Woolston is to be found there — once citizens of Eden.

Perhaps there are no country residences for fifty miles around, equaling in beauty and cost that of Mr. C. B. Mendenhall and Mr. Conway Rhodes—with the most substantial barns and out-houses, in keeping with their splendid homes.

Mr. Rhodes built the first mill and store in Edenville, in 1857, bringing the lumber and goods from Iowa City, using very emphatic words at the sloughs, —so he reports.

The first postmaster was Mr. Isaac Sanford, who afterward kept hotel on East Main street, and had a shoe shop also. His name appears among the first Justices in the township.

The first Fourth-of-July celebration was in 1858, when the little village was all excitement. Baskets and bundles went forward to the rustic tables, there was music by the choir, and an oration by Rev. Mr. Merrill of Jasper county. Zenas Bartlett was Grand Marshal, and the older settlers will remember of being marched around the mill and back to the grove in the hot sunshine—rather more fatigued than patriotic. There

was a splendid flag in the procession, and the beautiful Emma Tuffree, who died in 1862, sang the
national airs with the sweetness of a full-throated
lark, as she marched along with a few school girls.

Mr. Benson, who a few years later was killed by
lightning, was one of the company, and Martin Logan,
the first on the starry record of Eden's heroic dead.
Next, was Mr. Bartlett, who left wife and little
children and an aged father, but alone with his nurse,
died in a St. Louis hospital; then the merry-hearted
George Culver; Irving Benson, who was killed at
Champion Hills, nobly bearing the colors in that
ghastly highway from Jackson, Miss.; then the martyred prisoner, Simon Woolston, whose sweet, boyish face
will never be forgotten here; after him, Harry Nichols,
who went late to the army but died early at Alexan-
dria, after he had marched with "Sherman round to the
sea," and sank to sleep without a comrade to fold
the army blue over his brave heart. Tears fill my
eyes as I write of these soldier boys, for I knew them
well. They sleep in almost nameless graves, where
no loving sympathy can plant the myrtle and the rose,
or erect the enduring marble to their memories.

ORDER OF GOOD TEMPLARS.

This time-honored institution of temperance was
organized in 1859, and by its efficient labors has
entirely banished whisky-selling for miles around.
Among its charter members, who bore the brunt of
persecution in the good work, were Mr. F. T. Woolston,
Mr. John Jeroleman and lady, Charley Price, whose
gude-wife is one of the sweet singers of upper Eden,
and Mrs. Scotten, a very efficient officer in the order.
But alas! the banners of the lodge are trailed in
the dust, and the enterprise is among the things *that
were.*

In our notice of Eden, we must not overlook the

lively poetess of the "Star of Hope," Mrs. A. Bullock, or Mrs. Maggie Brewer, a contributor to the same.

Among those who came later to this township, who in a few years have become wealthy and prosperous, is Mr. D. Harmon, a highly gifted singer; Mr. A. Viles, Esq.; Mr. James Nichols, from Pennsylvania; and last, though not least on our list, Mr. T. Robb and Mr. J. B. Mendenhall.

STATE CENTER

Originally belonged to Eden and a part of Washington township, and was set off after the village of State Center reached nearly full stature. In the winter of 1863, about the first of December, State Center Station was dropped down upon the railroad track, and looked desolate and lonely enough the first winter, as there were but two or three houses besides those belonging to the Cedar Rapids and Missouri Railroad Company.

The oldest resident, we think, was Mr. William Barnes, who bought produce at the station—a very energetic man. Next, came Mr. John Anselme, the pioneer of French Grove, and built a hotel, or rather transported a building on wheels from the village of Marietta across the prairie ten miles. In the spring following, Mr. Bassett built a beautiful residence in the northern part of town, which being in an elevated position, was a sort of lighthouse for a long distance to tired travelers.

About this time it was noised about that State Center was *the* center of Iowa, the very pivot of the Hawkeye State. Lots had an upward tendency at this hub. Then came the Carpenters, men of capital and enterprise, from Sandwich, Ill. Soon, the firm of Shipman & Dobbins gave a new impetus to trade in that vicinity; next in order, the mechanics and artisans, that make up the bone and sinew of a town ; another hotel, kept by Mr. W. Greenfield, swung out good cheer to the passer-by ; and finally drug stores, furniture rooms, etc., stood coaxingly on the streets, to relieve the farmers of State Center and Eden of their spare cash.

TERRIBLE TORNADO.

On the 27th of June, 1865, there came up a terrible thunder storm from the west, with flashing lightning and roar of heaven's artillery, while the wind seemed to come like an avalanche, sweeping everything before it. Mr. T. M. Carpenter had a store of dry goods, and occupied the back part as a home for his family ; there was a rush, then came a terrific crash, the cries of little children mingled with groans and sobs from the inmates, and the storm beating down upon their heads. On examination, it was found the whole structure had blown down, one of the timbers striking a little girl about seven years of age, and the stove in falling over had inflicted some dreadful burns upon the babe of a few months. All had received more or less injuries, the goods in the building were scattered about the debris and ruin, and bearing their wounded children in their arms, the terror-stricken parents sought shelter at the nearest house as soon as possible. The little girl died the next morning, in spite of medical assistance ; she was attended by Dr. Waters of Marshalltown, through whose skill and the careful nursing of the mother, the infant finally recovered, after a great deal of suffering.

The strange freaks of the wind—which, in its peaceful moments, is so like an infant's breath—were noticeable. Heavy sticks of timber, and long and unmanageable boards, were seen flying through the air in every direction ; chips of wood and bunches of the blow-weed were playing cross-fire ; while the dust and fragments of brick and stone about the buildings elsewhere filled the atmosphere to such an extent, that it seemed as if a heavy garment had been dropped down between heaven and earth. A wagon box was carried a long distance without the wheels, a wash-tub was moored away out on the prairie without mortal hands, and pails, pots and billets of wood danced a jig outside of the houses to the music of the storm.

PRESENT PROSPERITY.

There is scarcely a town in the State that has made such advance in wealth and prosperity as State Center. In a little more than three years it has grown from a hamlet of two families to a population of five hundred; has dry goods stores, millinery shops, manufactories of harness, shingles, shoes, etc. ; with a flourishing Good Templars' Lodge. A large public school-house has been built the past season and furnished with a beautiful toned bell, and walnut desks, blackboards, and everything to make the building comfortable for student and teacher. Most of the inhabitants were from Sandwich, Northern Illinois, and brought with them much of the energy and go-ahead-a-tive-ness of that region.

The farms in the vicinity of State Center are scarcely equaled for good crops, and their neat, thrifty appearance, especially Mr. Bowen's, Van Pelt's and L. Brown, Esq. Once, Mr. Brown's farm was considered the jumping-off place on the wide sea of grass beyond. John O. Groat's house upon the Scottish headlands was not more welcome to the mariner than this farm-house, with its stately wheat stacks and droves of pigs and chickens, was to the wayfarer upon the billowy undulation of that far-stretching prairie.

State Center has an exceedingly pleasant location viewed from the westward. It will soon be a fine business point, as there is no town of any size in the whole region from Marshall to Nevada. There are already two large warehouses, and an elevator in process of erection for the storage of grain, etc., and a Methodist church is talked of the coming season. Shipman & Dobbins have established a newspaper, and with their characteristic energy, it will be of benefit to the village. There is also a small job office, doing some very creditable work in the publishing line.

Mr. J. Price is supplying with dressed lumber a large region of country, and nice comfortable farm-houses are dotting the prairie at every point of the compass. Mr. Walker is also in the same business, gladdening the eyes of new-comers with that important article, so necessary to a new home — cheap pine lumber.

Emigrants are coming in every day to State Center and the township.

WASHINGTON TOWNSHIP

Is situated west of Timber Creek and south of Mari-etta, the Waterloo and Marshalltown road passing through it on to Edenville, Peoria and Desmoines. It has some very fine timber in it; Starry and Bear Groves being the largest bodies in the township. It is an elevated plateau, excepting the northern portion, and contains beautiful farms in a high state of cul-tivation. There are a good many sheep in this vicinity, and, thanks to the factory in Marshalltown, the wool commands a fair price or can be exchanged for cloth.

Henry Starry was the first settler in this township, having moved from Iowa county in 1852. He came in with wagons, bringing with him his stock, nails and farming utensils, and even the flour for a year's use. His daughter Mary remembers driving the old cows along, as she walked a good deal of the way. He entered the land called Starry's Grove, also his farm, and built his cabin westward of the timber. The next family was a Mr. Miller, a brother-in-law of Mr. Starry. They all went a hundred miles to mill, fought wolves, killed rattlesnakes, broke up nature's green sward, welcomed new comers, heard the pro and con of the Marietta war, and gradually grew rich and prosperous.

Among these early settlers were Mr. Gotham and the Manwarings from New York, also Mr. Wickersham and Mr. Myers of Bear Grove. We will say, *en passant*, that Mrs. Myers is a model farmer. She hires help to do the housework, and with a Bloomer dress made of bed-ticking, may be seen hauling wood, driving a reaper or sulky plow, and is one of the most successful managers in the county. She has been known to go down to Iowa City for a load of lumber, accompanied only by her little boy, camping out, boiling her teakettle by the roadside, and taking care of the team herself.

We would recommend her to the notice of the New York Tribune and the American Agriculturist, for she far outshines their pet female farmers in Central New York. We must admire her self-reliance, although some may question her taste.

PRAIRIE FIRES.

If we should wish to get up an entertainment upon a grand scale for an Eastern audience, a prairie fire would be the most entertaining. A fire could sweep for about ten miles from the north down through into Jasper county in almost a direct line without the least interruption, as the western half of both Washington and Jefferson townships are prairie uplands, with only a farm to break in occasionally on its course.

At one time Mr. S. Manwaring was aroused by the crackling and roaring of the fire, and on looking out saw the haystacks in a blaze, with danger to the house and stable. At once all hands were set to work to carry water, and finally, by the help of wet blankets and carpets, they saved a part of the hay and buildings. But hundreds of tons of hay are lost every year in Iowa from fires often carelessly lit by the pipe of a passing hunter, or boys bent on mischief.

One night, Mr. Gotham was awakened by the light of a coming fire, and in a costume nearly Georgian, he succeeded in getting a furrow ploughed around his buildings, but there was a hen-roost in one corner of the yard where the fire got up some strange *dissolving* views within, for the poultry disappeared, then appearing in the morning tailless, with their wings badly burnt.

The railroad passes along the banks of Linn creek, a beautiful stream twenty-six miles in length, which meanders through the long grass of this prairie up to its source in Minerva township. A singular accident happened to the cars not far from Mr. A. H. Stone's. A bridge had become damaged by a freshet; the locomotive passed over, however, but the baggage and passenger cars went down into the water. This was in the darkness of the night, the cars overturning with heated stoves, burning lamps and sleeping passengers, yet the good God took care that none were hurt. Some of the cars were badly damaged, and the mails with the terror-stricken travelers had an involuntary bath.

Linn creek is a haunted stream. On the 9th of April, 1867, a young lady with her father, Mr. Hudson, was drowned about two miles west from Marshalltown. Miss Hudson attempted to cross on the submerged bridge, but the horse lost his foothold upon the plank, there being no railing, and both fell into the water. Her father, attracted by the screams of the daughter and the shouts of quite a party assembled near, not one of whom could swim, plunged in, but lost his hold upon a bunch of willows to which he had clung for support, and not being a good swimmer they both sank to rise no more.

A Mr. Algoyee was also drowned some years since not far from Le Grand highway bridge, in attempting a bath. Near here Mrs. Ed. Lockwood and Mrs. H. Nash had a narrow escape about seven years ago. Their horse had become frightened by covered wagons and kept obstinately backing, till he reached the bank, when he tipped the buggy over with its human freight into the current, excepting Mrs. Nash and child who fortunately alighted a moment before. Mrs. Lockwood and her little daughter struggled in the icy water, it being in March. She succeeded in holding her child up from the stream with one hand, while clinging with the other to the willows, and was finally rescued from her peril by the Pike's Peak travelers, who had caused the mischief. The only damage done was to the buggy and harness, and the sinking of a basket of vegetables which the party had made the journey to obtain. But we will follow the windings of the ill-fated stream back to Washington.

Situated in a beautiful grove is the home of John Haynes who came here in 1854. He is of Scottish descent, and with the determination, characteristic of that earnest people, he bravely went through the hardships of the West without flinching. His brother Thomas is his neighbor, and a thrifty farmer. The Haynes, with Mr. Starry, have been pillars in the Protestant Methodist Church in this vicinity, and Mr. John Haynes was also very instrumental in keeping up the Good Templar organization.

About seven miles from Marshall, is a station in this township called Cedar Cross Roads. There has been something done towards laying out a town by Mr. F. A. Stone.

Among the wealthy men of Washington whom we have failed to notice, is Mr. John McCord, Mr. Wilson, who drew the splendid silk quilt at the Orphans'

Fair, Mr. Wyatt, and Mr. Thayer—all good citizens.
This township is every way adapted to sustain a large
population.

JEFFERSON.

This township is bounded on the north by Timber
Creek township, eastward by Greencastle, south by the
Jasper line, and on the west by a township not named,
being all prairie south of Washington. The road from
Marshalltown to Newton, passes through Jefferson,
winding through the lanes and door-yards of the
"Kentucky settlement," and finally goes out among
the knolls of the southern edge, till a wagon, seen
in the distance, from Mr. Archerd's, has the appearance of a big fat spider crawling slowly along on
the sky's edge.

The earliest settler was Mr. William Powers, who
entered his land in 1852, giving his name to the grove
and farm. This grove is on the south branch of
Timber creek, which heads westward nearly to the
Eden line in a romantic little lakelet of about an acre
of clear pellucid water. Here are brandts and wild
geese in early spring in great numbers, to attract
sportsmen.

Mr. Powers' family suffered many privations, as they
were obliged to go to Oskaloosa to mill—no church,
and their nearest neighbor four or five miles distant.
Mr. Putnam is an excellent citizen, living near the
Kentucky settlement, which in 1855 was opened up
by four farms, the land being first entered by Mr.
Currens. Mr. Rogers was one of the largest proprie-
tors—had a farm of two hundred acres. And Mr.
Archerd who now keeps the Union House, was also
an early settler, and has grown rich and prosperous
here on his fruitful farm.

This year, 1855, also saw a family settle upon the
south edge of the township by the name of Hoppin.
They were from New Jersey, he, a dry goods clerk,

the wife, a young woman who had seen better days, and two little children. He had only about five hundred dollars, but seeing the beautiful prairie in this part of Jefferson, bought an unfenced claim, with a cabin. He also purchased a yoke of oxen, but being inexperienced, his crop of 1856 proved to be a little corn, a few pumpkins, and perhaps a peck of garden beans. The cold winter of 1856–7 coming on, he attempted to keep his oxen and cow from freezing, but was taken down with typhoid fever and died without medical attendance. Soon after, the cattle died, and this brave woman with her children lived alone that terrible winter, with but very little additions to the winter's store of provision. There was nothing to buy, the emigration was so heavy that year, and if there had been, she had no money. She wore her husband's coats and boots, obtained fuel, dug snow drifts, lived on parched corn for bread, and did not see a cup of tea or coffee for eighteen months. Any one but a heroine would have become disheartened and begged out of Iowa, but she clung to the farm, and the next year she raised a good crop without a fence, the neighbors lending a team, and in six years she sold the farm for eighteen hundred dollars, and with the proceeds of a year's produce, she went back to the Camden and Amboy State, rejoicing in her self-reliance.

The Desmoines and Cedar Rapids telegraph, which passed through Newton and Marshalltown, had its line swung on tall cottonwood posts through here and Timber Creek, but it did not pay much of a dividend other than outgoes, and it was discontinued, the people burning the supports for firewood, after the line was taken down.

Mr. Schettler, a very enterprising stock dealer, settled in this township twelve years since, and has become wealthy in the business. He was from Maysville, Ky., and helped a great deal in carrying on the enterprises of roads, schools, etc., in the settlement. They have several fine school houses, larger than is generally seen in country neighborhoods. This township has excellent soil, some good timber, and is every way a good point for farmers to settle in.

The names of the soldiers from Jefferson who sleep in Southern graves, are Clarington Poynes, who enlisted in the Second Cavalry, and William King. They were brave, good boys, and were sadly missed from the fireside and community. There were several who were discharged from inability and disease.

HUNTING PARTIES.

The prairie in the western portion has been noted for hunting parties, with dogs, guns, snack-baskets, and bottles of *corn coffee.* There is a tradition extant of one party who went to the head of Timber creek and killed seven hundred and eight chickens. These broiled, with hot rolls, and a cup of good Java, is a dish fit for a king. No wonder our prairies present such attractions to English and other sportsmen. Last season a large party of hunters from Buffalo visited this section. They were highly pleased with their success, and as our railroad facilities are increasing, no doubt in a few years our lovely plains will receive a full share of the summer tourists who journey for health and comfort.

Mr. George Wills, with a party of five, went beyond Powers' Grove and killed three hundred and eleven chickens in one day, returning to town with their wagon loaded down with game. If this slaughtering should go on long at a time, the question is, where would the chickens be? unless the Darwinian theory be true, that animals can be made from vegetable matter, and chickens could be manufactured from brown grass and Timber creek water.

CONSERVATISM.

Jefferson township has politically been rather conservative, and a few went so far as to tease their neighbors by hanging butternuts on the telegraph poles and on the latch-string of their doors, but there has been quite a change of public sentiment recently, and the fossil remnants of conservatism are disappearing under a growth of free and enlightened opinion

The Methodists and Disciples both have meetings in the school-houses, but on the lower edge of the township there are a good many Germans, a very industrious people, who having grown quite wealthy in a few years, now think of uniting with those of Malaka township in Jasper county, and building a church edifice of their own near the line of Jefferson. We believe they are Lutherans, and hold service in their own language. The German pastor from Newton ministers to their spiritual need when he can be spared from his own parish.

Just this side of the Kentucky settlement may be found a Mr. Fuller, who with his amiable wife dispenses hospitality to the stranger, yet sighs for the "Kentucky home far away."

LIBERTY.

Liberty township occupies the extreme north-western corner of Marshall county, has a number of small streams that form the north fork of the Minerva, and others tributary to the Iowa, and has a fine body of timber in Illinois Grove, the main portion of which is in Liberty, a few acres only crossing the Hardin line. Coal is found near this grove in abundance. It is a pity capitalists leave this enterprise so to languish. Timber is in close proximity; the fencing is excellent, and the crops are always good. There are fine fields of sorghum and broom corn, as well as all the other staple products of the soil.

13

Mr. William Howard is quite an old settler, coming in 1855. He is favorably known as a faithful officer in the Board of Supervisors, and is an excellent neighbor and citizen.

Among other good farmers, we are slightly "acquaint" with Mr. Mandeville Colwell, a Scotchman by birth, and who brought to this neighborhood all the thrift and intelligence characteristic of that glorious people, the countrymen of Burns and Wallace, of Bruce and Kit North.

Mr. Holcomb, a brother-in-law of Dr. Waters of Marshalltown, is well known in this section. Also a Mr. Wm. McCormick, who left a good home, wife and little children, and gave his life for the nation, after some months' service.

Mr. Ingledew is often mentioned as a prominent citizen of Liberty, and a Mr. Davis. Mr. William Bevins came here as early as 1851—has a good farm, and Bevins' Grove is known for many miles. Mr. Charles Tucker has quite a pleasant little inn that might be called the "half-way" house, as it stands so near the line that he may be counted a citizen of both Story and Marshall.

Quite a heavy wind passed over this township and Bangor in 1859. It was on a May Sabbath afternoon. The day had been very warm, and at 4 o'clock there rose in the north-west a huge black cloud with a sea green edge, which rapidly came to the zenith. The wind came "tearing down" from that quarter, sweeping over the timber and twisting the trees like whips. In crossing the fields it cleaned the young corn right out of the soil as with a scraper, whirling the sand into winrows like stacks of hay.

It was the same storm that caused the loss of life in New Providence and Camanche. Mrs. Groff, a lady who lived on a farm in this township, says it was almost impossible, by the united strength of herself and husband, to keep a western door from bursting the hinges and blowing down.

They have a post office at Illinois Grove. Among the settlers who used to meet at their firesides and talk over the Marietta war, the probability of Marshalltown being the capital, and went to mill to Xenia, and to church in a small school-house at the south-east corner of Liberty, were William Spence, Esq., and William Stough.

We believe the first Justice was George Magee; and after some trials of pioneer life in Minerva township came Mr. Elder and settled here.

Liberty township gave a good account of herself all through the war, and did nobly for the Sanitary funl and the Orphans' Home Fair. They are favored here by the preaching of Rev. Mr. Eberhart of Albion. There are a number of good school-houses, but if the people would unite and build a church in this vicinity it would be a fine thing for this section. People coming into a new country look out for church spires.

MARSHALL COUNTY.

We now resume our theme of the county's growth
and great development in the short time that has
elapsed since its settlement. In population, taking
for our data the census of 1865, and the immense
emigration for the last two years, we have no hesi-.
tancy in placing it in round numbers at 12,000
Some idea of its wealth may be inferred from the
real estate sales, as shown by the recorder's book for
three months of the last year. They amount to
$212,600.

At State Center, Bangor, and more than all at Marshalltown, there is a heavy tide of wealth and population flowing in, that will *tell* soon in our business
tables and abstracts. Each hour, "prairie schooners"
are run upon our highways; besides, the cars bring a
a great many with settlers for Marshall county, showing that this is to be the home of a dense population.
We have scarcely an acre of waste land, and as the
crops never fail here, and the soil is of such remarka-
ble fertility, we have only to exclaim, "There is room
for all."

One farmer in Washington township has cleared
over twelve hundred dollars on eighty acres of land,
beside supporting his family handsomely. Many of
this kind of farmers, wealthy and energetic, sell out
and come to Marshalltown to live, having beautiful
homes, and adding to her wealth and prosperity. We
might mention Mr. J. H. McCord, from Washington,
Mr. Schettler, from Jefferson, Mr. Baldwin, Mr. Spark,
and others, from different townships, of whom we
have not space to speak particularly.

We take leave of the county by saying, that aside
from the partiality of the judgment of a citizen, it is
one of the most desirable places for a residence, and
that *her* Capital should be the Capital of Iowa.

Taking up the pen we write of MARSHALLTOWN the metropolis, and the most enterprising city in Iowa of its size. With a population of four thousand, it has erected over two hundred buildings the past year, and has as many more in progress at this writing, July, 1867. It has a skating park, churches, town halls, four miles of sidewalk, factories, foundries, warehouses, a splendid bank, and other public buildings, which would do honor to any town, besides solid brick stores, hotels, and a large and commodious depot.

Sleight & Downer paid for wheat, $195,864; and for live hogs, $69,300. Their cash receipts were $313,363.50. Their sales of agricultural implements amounted to $84,163.97.

Willigrod & Geier bought 65,000 bushels of wheat; Mr. Abraham Stanley, another heavy dealer in grain, probably did as much business, though we have not the exact amount.

Binford, Morgan & Co.'s account of sales for wheat, reads $150,000.20 from their books, and in their new store they will probably do a larger business the present season.

The aggregate amount of sales at our dry goods stores, stands exactly at $307,000.

Banbury & Caswell, grocers, did a heavy business of $50,000 last year. They are both good men, and very enterprising, although Mr. Caswell is generally poring over law books instead of working behind the counter. They both served in the Union army with distinction.

Col. Jack's figures (at the old stand of S. Lacy), as given by him in a rough estimate, were $40,000, in eleven months.

There are others which can give as good showing; among them, are Ginder & Co.

Berthold & Smith, according to their capital, have done a good business the past year.

Turner, Stone & Co., hardware dealers, foot up, in receipts, $65,000.

W. K. Smith sold $125,000 worth of lumber; Stocking & Price, $50,000, and D. B. Cunningham, as much more.

We remark, in passing, that the only drawback our city has, is the need of a large educational institution. Though our public school-house is commodious, costing about ten thousand dollars, and our select schools of a high character, yet we have no seminary building, or college, in our midst. Prof. Williams and Miss A. Gifford have excellent schools in operation, but these are too crowded and need more room.

Our city is under the charge of Col. B. W. Johnson as Mayor, who was one of the most able and accomplished officers in the Sixteenth Army Corps. He has been elected to serve the county in the next Legislature as our representative to the lower house, with his genial colleague to the Senate, W. S. Rice, Esq., both receiving rousing majorities.

Incidentally we have mentioned the most of our leading business houses, with perhaps the exception of Mr. S. Lacy's splendid furniture rooms; Lee, Bromley & Co., a dry goods firm which commenced operations here in 1865, from Kenosha, Wis., reliable, gentlemanly dealers in every way; also the splendid grocery house of Hill, Liddle & Pollock, just opened on North Main street; Abbot & Co.'s hardware store; and not forgetting the " old Galena stand-by" Willard & Grumme, leather dealers, who have the largest roll of workmen in the city.

All of our County officers are most deserving men —none more faithful than our time-honored citizens, Harry Gerhart, Esq., and J. L. Williams.

IN THE COURTS.

An appeal from Justice Parker, who, by the way, reads Byron as well as Kent, sends us before Judge Chase of the District Court, a heavy, substantial framed man, with a forehead like Webster, and a keen grey eye, who watches a turn in the case with great eagerness as there is no jury before him. At his right on a bench sits District Attorney Bradley, who is too handsome for a very successful lawyer, languidly reading the Times, with an occasional look at Street, the counsel for a client, who twists facts into a terrible snarl. Street seems attempting a cover for his fox, which Brown, the legal bloodhound, is hunting down with a keen scent. He raps out very disturbing questions to the witness with the right forefinger upon his left palm.

We turn to Boardman, with his analytic brain and cold, impassioned face, who is talking to Henderson. The gallant senator has but a moment before touched his beaver to a lady, and is listening with a dreamy look to the conversation, betraying more interest just now in the fair sex than the legal points of any case.

Griswold, neat and gentlemanly, a safe counselor in trouble, is examining briefs carefully at the table. Col. Johnson, another of our first class lawyers, bluff and hearty, looking every inch a soldier, is also reading papers by the wholesale. Binford, and Mercer, with lesser lights of the profession, are mingled in the tableaux, making an array of legal talent every way creditable to the county.

Judge Lampman, of an excellent family, has been here some time among our lawyers, and is one of the most earnest, hard-working officers in Marshall.

Emerging from the court house we pass Drs. Sherwood and Lang, to hear a stir of scientific words on the air.

Coming home. we close our record with a glow of pride in Marshalltown and the County. Proud of her material prosperity, proud of the intelligence and virtue of our citizens, proud of that motto "Excelsior," she has written on her banners, we dream of a glorious future for Marshalltown, the Queen of the Iowa valley—one of the largest cities in the State and the Great Northwest.

MARSHALLTOWN

BUSINESS DIRECTORY.

DRY GOODS AND MERCHANDISE.

Lee, Bromley & Co., two clerks, corner of Main and Court streets.
B K. Adams, three clerks, Main street.
Wells S. Rice, three clerks, Main street.
Whealen & Harvey, three clerks, Main street.
Woodworth & Whitton, three clerks, Main street.
David Parrett, two clerks, Main street.
Loree & Wasson, one clerk, Main street.
Harper & Co., one clerk, Main street.

GROCERY STORES.

G. W. Ginder, two clerks, Main street.
D. Heasty, one clerk, Main street.
Duguid & Fuller, Main street.
Berthold & Smith, Main street.
Norton & Gillespie, Main street.
Johnson & Waters, one clerk, Center street.
Dunton & Nicodemus, two clerks, Center street.
J. T. Jack & Co., Main street, wholesale and retail dealers, two
    clerks, Center street.
Banbury & Caswell, wholesale and retail dealers, two clerks,
    Main street.

CLOTHING AND FURNISHING GOODS.

Moses Stern, two clerks, Main street.
Steifle & Co., two clerks. Main street.
Chas. Birnbaum, one clerk, Main street.
A. Loomis, one clerk, Main street.
Meyer & Gump, one clerk, Main street.
D. Hurst & Co., one clerk, Main street.

MILINERY AND FANCY GOODS.

Mrs. M. C. Bailey, Main street.
Mrs. N. M. Holt, Main street.
Misses E. B. and M. A. Lang, Main street.
Miss Maria Collins, Main street.

14

BOOTS AND SHOES.

S. Ambruster, manufacturer, store in his splendid brick block, four
hands employed, Main street.
G. W. Peet, manufacturer, four hands, Main street.
C. Woods & Son, one clerk, Main street.
W. W. Miller, one clerk, Main street.

DRUG STORES.

Drs. Taylor & Barnhart, Main street.
Mabie, Roe & Co., one clerk, Main street.
Dr. George Glick, wholesale and retail, has three clerks, and oc-
cupies a perfect bijou of a salesroom, the finest west of the
Mississippi.

FRUIT & CONFECTIONERY.

William Pentland, one clerk, Main street.
Ehle & Collyer, one clerk, Main street.
D. W. Tate, one clerk, Main street.
S. Keuner, one clerk, Main street.

PROVISION AND FEED STORES.

Forney & Thayer, one clerk, Main street.
Mark Varnum, Main street, does a heavy business also in this line.

MEAT MARKETS.

A. Jenkins, one clerk, Main street.
Shorthill & Co., Main street.   Thomas Clark, Main street.

BOOKS AND STATIONERY.

C. N. Shaw & Co., one clerk, Main street.
M. Rosenbaum, one clerk, Main street.

JEWELLERS.

C. Miller, one clerk, Main street.
Warrick & Speer, one clerk, Main street.

DENTISTRY.

Dr. Wm. H. Marvin, Main street.   Dr. Knepper, Glick's block.
Dr. D. E. Rickey, Main street.

PICTURE AND ART GALLERIES.

Baum & Datesman, Main street.   Miss Shaw, Union Hotel.
J. Lee Knight, Main street, who did the extensive business of $5,000
last year.

PAINTERS, AND FRESCO ARTISTS.

A. P. Hogle, Main street.
Heighton & Bundy, Center street.
E. F. Dean, West Main street.

LIVERY AND SALE STABLES.

Green & Beasley, Chestnut street.
N. V. Speer, Center street.

HOTELS.

McLain House, Station street ; J. W. McLain, Proprietor.
Marshal House, Main street; C. W. Sherman, Proprietor.
City Hotel, Main street ; E. E. Shaw, Proprietor.
Union House, Center street ; A. Hall, Proprietor.
Miller's Hotel, Court street ; S. S. Miller, Proprietor.

Another hotel would add greatly to our advantage as a city, especially through the spring emigration.

DINING SALOONS.

St. James Restaurant, Marshall & Quick, Main street.
Excelsior Restaurant, Chas. Epeneter, Main street.

AUCTIONEERS.

Rhodes & Snider, Center street.   M. Mundsell, Main street.

MANUFACTORIES.

Henderson & Co.
Woodbury & Son, twenty-five men, near Depot.
E. W. Lockwood, six men, near Depot.
Chester Heald, three men, near Depot.
S. Lacey, four men, Main street.
Wm. East, four men, Main street.
Hodge & Canfield, two men, near Depot.
Shaw, Andrews & Co., two men, Center street.
Wm. H. Calhoun, West Main street.
Landsberry & Miller, Flour Mills.
J. M. Sherwood, Flour Mills.

DRAYMEN.

Sanford & Curkhuff, Main street.   I. J. Sanford, Main street.
De Loss, Main street.

BARBERS.

Dick Ward, Main street.   J. C. Beverly, Main street.

BAKERS.

Brenor & Engehart, Main street.   F. Kenner.

LEATHER, HARNESS AND SADDLERY.

Willard & Grumme, ten men, Main street.
G. Schettler, three men.

HARDWARE AND TIN STORES.

Turner, Stone & Co., six men, Main street.
Abbott & Knisely, five men, Main street.
Loree & Wasson, one man, Main street.
P. Holcomb, one man, Main street.

BLACKSMITHS.

Bishop & Scager, two hands employed, Main street.
Johnson & Snider, two hands employed, Center street.
Walter Billings, two hands employed, Main street.
Wm. E. Vickery & Co., Locust street.
Nash & Wann, Center street.

WAGON MAKERS.

II. D. Wiley, two hands, Main street.
A. C. Strickland, two hands, Center street.
D. E. Snider, two hands, Center street.
Nash & Wann, two hands, Center street.

LUMBER DEALERS.

Smith Bros., near Depot.   Price & Stocking, near Depot.
D. W. Cunningham, near Depot.

GRAIN ELEVATORS, STORAGE, AGRICULTURAL IMPLE-MENTS.

Sleight & Downer, Station street.
Binford, Morgan & Co., East Main street.
Willigrod & Geier, Station street.
Abram Stanley, Station street.

FURNITURE DEALERS.

William East, Main street.   S. Lacey, south side Main street.
Dunham & Cronkleton, Broom Warehouse.

ARCHITECTS.

Col. W. Legg, Center street.
A. White.   B. F. Dean.   S. Kline.

ATTORNEYS.

Boardman & Brown, Woodbury's block.
Henderson & Binford, Woodbury's block.
J. H. Bradley, Woodbury's block.
J. W. Street, over Glick's Drug Store.
B. W. Johnson, over Glick's Drug Store.
Obed Caswell, Woodbury's block.
L. W. Griswold, Main street.
J. M. Sherwood, Main street.
J. N. Parker, Main street.
W. E. Snelling, Main street.

REAL ESTATE AGENTS.

Johnson & Giddings, Court house.
McCracken, Cooper & Weatherly, Court house.
Boardman & Brown, Main street.

PHYSICIANS AND SURGEONS.

Dr. Wm. C. Cummings, Main street.
Dr. E. J. B. Slater, Center street.   Dr. A. Lang, Main street.
Dr. A. J. Sherwood, Main street.   Dr. W. B. Waters, Main street.
Dr. L. E. Holt, Main street.   Dr. J. Lawrence, Main street.

MUSIC TEACHERS.

Prof. J. D. Montgomery and Lady, Main street.
Prof. H. H. Heighton, Center street.
Miss Nettie Cole.   Mrs. A. McClure.

Silver Brass Band, H. Gerhart, Leader.

COUNTY OFFICERS.

T. P. LAMPMAN, *County Judge.*
H. GERHART, *Treasurer.*   J. L. WILLIAMS, *Clerk.*
THOMAS McCRACKEN, *Sheriff.*   A. J. COOPER, *Recorder.*

CITY OFFICERS.

B. W. JOHNSON, *Mayor.*   THOS. MERCER, *Treasurer.*
J. LEE KNIGHT, *Recorder.*   M. MUNSELL, *Marshal.*
G. GLICK,   A. ABBOTT,   } *Councilmen.*
N. WILLARD,   J. H. McLAIN, }

STATEMENT OF BENEVOLENT CONTRIBUTIONS.

Amount donated by Marietta for Aid Societies and Orphans' Home Fair, $2,340.

Amount raised by the Marshall County Auxiliary Aid Society, for the Dubuque Sanitary Fair, $2,800.57.

M. E. GRIFFITH, *Sec.*   MRS. N. L. BUNCE, *Pres.*
JULIA LEACH, *Treas.*

Whole amount of proceeds of Orphans' Home Fair, Marshalltown, $16,000.

Whole amount given by Marshall County for sanitary supplies at points South, $4,708.27.

Net proceeds of the Marshalltown Orphans' Home Society, $997.23.

MRS. N. HAMILTON, *Sec.*   MRS. NETTIE SANFORD, *Pres.*
MRS. M. EAST, *Treas.*   MRS. GEORGE WHEALEN, *V.Pres.*

Amount raised from Tableaux (by Mrs. M. A. Boardman and Mrs. N. Hamilton), for Orphans' Home Fair, $216.

STATEMENT

Of Monies invested in some of the principal Buildings finished in Marshalltown, November, 1867.

Wells Rice's splendid brick block, 40 by 80 feet, three stories, $15,000. John Crellin, Architect.

Abbott & Knisely — brick block, 22 by 50 feet, two stories, $5,000.

E. Willigrod, Esq. — mansion, Rhenish style of architecture, Mansard roof, modern improvements, $14,000. B. F. Dean, Architect.

J. L. Williams — mansion, architecture of the Elizabethan period, $11,000. G. F. Kline, Architect.

Hon. G. M. Woodbury — mansion, finished recently, Gothic style, $10,000.

Hon. H. E. J. Boardman — mansion, union of the Tudor and Elizabethan styles, $12,000.

Hon. T. E. Brown — elegant mansion, iron and stone facings, Elizabethan style, $12,000.

C. W. FRACKER,

General Insurance Agent

AND NOTARY PUBLIC,

AT THE FIRST NATIONAL BANK,

OF MARSHALLTOWN, IOWA.

REPRESENTING

$40,000,000.00 CASH CAPITAL.

Fire, Inland, Life, Accident,

AND LIVE STOCK INSURANCE.

LIST OF COMPANIES.

Mutual Life, New York,.....................	$22,000,000 00
Accident, Columbus, O.,.....................	1,000,000 00
Live Stock, Hartford,........	500,000 00
Railway Passenger, Hartford,.................	304,800 00
Ætna Fire Insurance Co., Hartford,..	4,273,269 81
Home Fire Insurance Co., New York,.......	3,645,388 87
Underwriters' Agency, New York,...........	3,364,957 78
Lorillard Fire, New York,....................	1,436,540 27
Manhattan Fire, New York,...	1,052,128 10
Corn Exchange Fire, New York,........... ..	501,095 79
North America Fire, Philadelphia,...........	1,731,515 14
Enterprise Insurance Co., Cincinnati,.......	1,000,000 00

$40,809,695 76

HILL, LIDDLE & POLLOCK,
DEALERS IN
Dry Goods, Groceries,
FISH, SALT, WOODEN WARE,
Wall and Window Paper, Curtain Fixtures, Oil Cloths,
STATIONERY, ETC.,
North Main Street, half block east of Bank,
MARSHALLTOWN, IOWA.

Having recently built our Store, and filled it with a stock of New Goods, for which we paid cash, thus being able to obtain them at the lowest market price, we now solicit the patronage of cash purchasers, believing we can furnish them with goods at very low prices.

Please call, examine our stock, and learn our prices.

Butter, Eggs, etc., taken in exchange for Goods.
HILL, LIDDLE & POLLOCK.

QUAKER CITY STORE.
DR. GEORGE WHEALAN,
DEALER IN
Dry Goods, Hats and Caps,
GROCERIES, ETC.,
Two Doors from Center Street,
MARSHALLTOWN, IOWA.

MARSHALL HOUSE,

C. W. SHERMAN, Proprietor.

MARSHALLTOWN, - - - IOWA.

Free Omnibus to and from the Cars. Good Stabling attached.
(160)

JOHN TURNER & CO.,

Wholesale and Retail Dealers in

HARDWARE,

STOVES, IRON, STEEL, NAILS,

Agricultural Implements,

TIN, SHEET IRON AND COPPER WARE.

Agents for the "Stewart Cook Stove," and "Studebaker South Bend Wagons."

JNO. TURNER. }
C. W. STONE. }

Marshalltown, Iowa.

THE GORDEN

WASHING MACHINE,

FOR SALE BY

WM. C. PAGE,

At the Store of B. K. Adams,

WHERE MACHINES CAN BE SEEN.

In every Family where the Machines have been used, they give entire satisfaction.

The following, from an old citizen of Marshalltown, now of Cedar Rapids, speaks for itself:

"I have used the Gorden Washing Machine in my family for the last year, and find that it saves much labor, and does not get out of order."

MRS. E. E. LEACH.

State and County Rights for Sale.

(161)

LEE & BROMLEY,

DEALERS IN

Dry Goods, Groceries,

BOOTS AND SHOES,

Hats, Caps, and Ready Made Clothing,

MARSHALLTOWN, - - IOWA.

BINFORD BRO'S & MORGAN,

DEALERS IN

AGRICULTURAL IMPLEMENTS

Of every Description.

MARSHALLTOWN, - - - IOWA.

Keep constantly on hand the very best Wagons, Plows, Seed Sowers, Reapers, Mowers, Threshers, Cultivators, etc., etc.

BANBURY & CASWELL,

DEALERS IN HEAVY AND LIGHT

Groceries, Crockery,

CIGARS, TOBACCO, ETC.,

Main Street, opposite the Public Square,

MARSHALLTOWN, - - IOWA.

CASH PAID FOR BUTTER AND EGGS.

MARSHALL'S

RESTAURANT,

Corner Main and Second Sts.,

UNDER BANK,

MARSHALLTOWN, - - - IOWA.

(162)

MARSHALL MARBLE WORKS.

WM. A. SMITH.   JOHN UTZ.

SMITH & UTZ,

DEALERS IN

Foreign and American Marble

Monuments,   Grave Stones,

TOMBS,   BUSTS,

Statues,   Medallions

FURNITURE MARBLE,

South Side of Main Street, East of Court House,

P. O. Address,
LOCK BOX 19.   MARSHALLTOWN, IOWA.

FIRST PREMIUMS.

Marshall County Fair, Sept. 26th and 27th, 1866.
Marshall County Fair, Sept. 25th, 26th and 27th, 1867.
Hardin County Fair, Oct. 10th and 11th, 1866.
Tama County Fair, Oct. 3d and 4th, 1866.
Tama County Fair, Oct. 10th, 11th and 12th, 1867.
Iowa County Fair, Oct. 9th, 10th and 11th, 1867.
Iowa Valley Fair, Oct. 18th and 19th, 1866.
Iowa Valley Fair, Sept. 18th, 19th and 20th, 1867.

Give us a call before purchasing, and we will guarantee satisfaction.

(163)

MARSHALL
WOOLEN MILLS
IN FULL OPERATION.

Seven Large Carding Machines,
480 SPINDLES, 10 LOOMS,
And all the necessary Machinery for Finishing.

WANTED.
100,000 POUNDS WOOL,
At the Highest Cash Price, in Cash, or in exchange for
GOODS OF OUR OWN MANUFACTURE.
G. M. WOODBURY & SON.

G. M. WOODBURY, *Pres.*   T. B. ABELL, *V. Pres.*   C. W. FRACKER, *Cashier.*

THE
FIRST NATIONAL BANK,
OF MARSHALLTOWN, IOWA.
DIRECTORS:
H. E. J. BOARDMAN.   THOS. B. ABELL.   G. M. WOODBURY.
GEO. GLICK.   DAVID PARRET.

Prompt attention given to Collections. Taxes paid in all Counties in Central Iowa.

ARCADE PHOTOGRAPH GALLERY,
MAIN STREET,
Near the Bank,   MARSHALLTOWN, IOWA.

Photographs, Ivorytypes,
AND AMBROTYPES,
In the Highest Style of Art. Coloring in India Ink, Oil,
or Water Colors.
J. LEE KNIGHT, Proprietor.
LOOK OUT FOR THE BIG SHOW CASE.
(164)

W. C. WOODWORTH. GEORGE WHITTON.

WOODWORTH & WHITTON,

Wholesale and Retail Dealers in

Dry Goods, Clothing,

BOOTS AND SHOES, NOTIONS ETC.

Corner of Main and Center Streets.

MARSHALLTOWN, IOWA

Look out for the Passenger Car.

HARVEY & DAVIS,

DEALERS IN

DRY GOODS.

Boots and Shoes, Hats, Caps, and Notions,

FIVE DOORS WEST OF THE BAN

J. W. HARVEY.
E. T. DAVIS.

Marshalltown. Iowa,

MRS. N. M. HOLT

HAS OPENED

NEW MILLINERY ROOMS,

(Formerly occupied by Mrs. Bailey,)

ON MAIN STREET,

MARSHALLTOWN. · · · *IOWA.*

DR. WM. H. MARVIN,

SURGEON DENTIST,

Office over W. W. Miller's Boot and Shoe Store,

MARSHALLTOWN, - - - **IOWA.**

ALL WORK WARRANTED.

(165)

W. S. RICE,

DEALER IN GENERAL

MERCHANDISE

Dry Goods,

Groceries,

Crockery,

BOOTS & SHOES,

Hats and Caps.

IN NEW SPLENDID BRICK BLOCK,

West Main Street, MARSHALLTOWN, IOWA.

Call and examine our Goods and learn our prices.

(166)

FURNITURE

Two Doors West of Marshall House,

MARSHALLTOWN,

IOWA.

ABBOTT & KNISELY,

Foreign and Domestic

HARDWARE

STOVES AND TIN WARE,

CUTLERY,

Sporting Apparatus, Plows, Wagon Material,

AGRICULTURAL IMPLEMENTS, &c.,

Opposite Marshall House,

MARSHALLTOWN, IOWA.

(168)

www.ingramcontent.com/pod-product-compliance
Lightning Source LLC
Chambersburg PA
CBHW020002030726
47500CB00002B/406